A SEA-

CHANGE

by Lois Gould

SIMON AND SCHUSTER : NEW YORK

DESIGNED BY IRVING PERKINS
MANUFACTURED IN THE UNITED STATES OF AMERICA

1   2   3   4   5   6   7   8   9   10

LIBRARY OF CONGRESS CATALOGING IN PUBLICATION DATA

GOULD, LOIS.
    A SEA-CHANGE.

    I. TITLE.
PZ4.G697SE   [PS3557.O87]   813'.5'4   76-13579

            ISBN 0-671-22326-7

For the B.,
as always

Males of *labroides dimidiatus* control the process of sex reversal within social groups. Each group consists of a male with a harem of females, among which larger individuals dominate smaller ones. The male in each harem suppresses the tendency of the females to change sex, by actively dominating them. Death of the male releases this suppression and the dominant female of the harem changes sex immediately.

Social Control of Sex Reversal in a Coral-Reef Fish
D. R. ROBERTSON
Zoology Department
University of Queensland
Australia, 1972

NOTE: *Labroides dimidiatus,* a member of the wrasse family commonly found in warm, reef-sheltered coastal areas, is related to certain cold-water wrasses native to the Atlantic Ocean, off New York. Another variety is known as the "sea wife."

Full fathom five thy father lies;
Of his bones are coral made;
Those are pearls that were his eyes:
Nothing of him that doth fade
But doth suffer a sea-change
Into something rich and strange.

The Tempest
WILLIAM SHAKESPEARE

Chapter I

JESSIE WATERMAN lay in a neatly folded pile beside her bed, a supplicant without a prayer, like a figure in one of those malignant contemporary sculptures that represent hell as a shock of recognition. Stone-aged woman staring at a color TV. Plasticine man with newspaper shoes, wine bottle and stained pants. Statutory rape (metal, acrylic, plaster and hair) in a battered hot rod with New Jersey plates. Robbery victim in blue bedroom.

In Jessie's case the artistic version would pay reverent attention to minute details: the knotted strips of torn nylon pantyhose binding wrists and ankles behind her back; the crossed bare feet, callused soles upturned like the tender parts of unfortunate animals.

She had been in this position long enough to plot a series of spectacular escapes. Rolling to the open window and hanging out like a lumpy package, bound fingers grasping the ledge. SOS notes written with a pencil grasped in the teeth and then spat out into the street. Whoever finds this I love you; please excuse handwriting.

But the nylon knots had been tied in such a way that Jessie's slightest move to free herself, or even to roll around with extreme caution, caused them to slip gently into a tighter hold upon her—a fine subtle paradox that no one would expect her to appreciate under the circumstances.

Useless to struggle, she decided finally, and sighed with relief, as if her victim's license had been automatically stamped VALID after a routine examination. Who was to say that non-struggling, like non-violence, wouldn't be better for both of them in the long run. (How very Jessie that was, always considerate, thinking not only of herself but also of her captor, the black gunman. Was it okay to call him B. G. from now on? They were on fairly intimate terms.)

Of course the plan worked. B. G., utterly tranquilized by her clever use of non-struggle, which he took as abject surrender, wandered off to seek his fortune elsewhere in the house. Whether he found riches beyond his wildest dreams, or only a couple of portable TVs and a digital clock, he might well be back any minute, lusting to commit some random atrocity in lieu of scrawling Kilroy or Stop Me Before I Kill More.

For now, though, Jessie, lulled by the sound of distant plunder, felt light-headed and perversely free. He'll take Robin's record player, she mused idly, and Roy's typewriter. The toaster? Maybe he won't bother—the warranty was up in February. Still, the first time the burglars came, they did take the toaster, and later Jessie, shopping for groceries, forgot and bought English muffins. At breakfast the next morning she had stood like a war orphan in their ransacked kitchen holding the split raw muffin halves. Helpless. Roy had laughed and muttered "crazy cunt" in the wise, affectionate tone he always adopted with that phrase. And Jessie had smiled her vague, radiant, model's smile in response, as if she hadn't quite heard, or else considered it a term of endearment. When-

14

ever Roy called her that in public, the combination of his tone and her smile made it easier for people to accept the premise that the Watermans were no less genuinely fond of each other than any of the rest of them.

Remembering the muffin incident now, and what Roy would say if it happened again, Jessie made an involuntary mental note: Check if toaster gone before shopping. Then she smiled at the implication. Only live people buy muffins by mistake.

After a while Jessie stopped feeling the slight tremors that marked the blazing of B. G.'s trail through the house. Detachment, like the numbness in her hands and feet, gradually filled her mind, sealing it off from the physical shocks of fear that had been coming in waves for the past hour. Already she could barely concentrate on the fear; only her muscles held on to it for dear life. Acting independently, her body had taken a vow the moment B. G. began to caress her breast with the gun. *I will not shit.*

Whatever happened now, she had that triumph, at least. She suppressed an urge to giggle. Wait till Roy hears; wait till I tell—

Roy Waterman was on his way home; was, in fact, within minutes of home. Wait till I tell— Suddenly Jessie saw a vivid snapshot of Roy being killed. Snap shot: B. G. firing his small black gun at point-blank range; Roy surprised at the front door; Roy falling; B. G. continuing to pack the contents of their former life into sturdy brown paper bags; Roy bleeding. Who should she call? Doctor. Lawyer. Police. Cleaner. *Crazy cunt.* She strained for the sound of footsteps now, or the scrape of Roy's key in the lock. Trying to conjure some brave and selfless act that she might yet commit, without hope of escape. A single image drifted toward her—elderly woman swathed in dark fur, gazing down. Jessie recognized her at once: Mrs. Straus, on the deck of the *Titanic,* shaking her patrician head at the upraised arms that reached toward her from the last lifeboat. Then another image appeared on the sloping deck. Husband, silent and unprotesting. I have lived with Mr. Straus for forty years, the woman announced in a pure silk voice. I'll not leave him now. It was not so much a sacrifice as a wifely duty; a silver tea ceremony. First class. *Mr. Straus said nothing, meaning, Of course.*

Well, Jessie had lived with Roy only ten years, and the last lifeboat was her own bound and silent body safely afloat here on the blue bedroom carpet. Silent: that was it. Jessie's brave and selfless act would be to yell. Scream! Shatter the silent safety zone. If she screamed . . . Roy would inherit the lifeboat, fleeing to safety, leaving her here with B. G. Would Mrs. Straus have gone down alone? Would Mr. Straus have let her? Stop, Roy! Don't Come In! *Armed Robber—Save Yourself!* Jessie sifted messages, weighing each phrase as if composing a night cablegram. Deferred rate—so much life per word. Framing the syllables with her lips, testing their strength. Once she stopped, horrified. Yell? I *can't.* But how would she explain that later? People would ask, Why didn't you yell? Why didn't you warn him? I was too frightened, she would say, tears welling comfortably in their accustomed places. I couldn't think, I was numb, I was helpless. You know how I am.

Everyone would nod and accept it. Reasonable, after all. *Everyone would say nothing, meaning, Of course.*

But of course it would be a lie. Jessie would have made a conscious choice—save me, not him. Let it happen, whatever it is. Let it happen *to him.* Or, if he's lucky, let him kill the other one. Or both of them, scuffling for the gun. Not my fault, not my responsibility; look, my hands were tied. I couldn't help it. Anyway, I hate Roy. (*Hate Roy?* She had never thought that before. She took it calmly.) If B. G. killed him I'd be free. Then B. G. would kill me too. I'd still be free. She repeated the sequence several times. It sounded right. Almost musical.

But what if Roy survived? If they both did? Roy himself surviving to ask—accuse—her: Why didn't you yell? You could have warned me! She would gaze at him blandly, tears in place. Me? she would say. I couldn't. You know how I am. Did he? *Of course.*

So she went on with her practicing. STOP ROY (STOP) SAVE YOURSELF (STOP). Silent scream, a tragedy prevented in one act. Let's run through it once more, Jessie: DON'T COME IN ROY STOP (STOP). Her throat was parched, searing; she felt the words packed down hard in her chest, rolled into a ball, squeezed dry. Loaded words, ready to be fired, and she had never fired a word in her life. But now she could hear them, rolling, bursting—dumdum words tearing jagged holes in the dark (STOP).

There was a sudden sharp sound, perhaps a click—a key? And then the explosion—in her throat?—a scream? Terrible noise tearing fierce jagged holes, black and red in the night. Dog barking somewhere; door opening somewhere; footsteps muffled and carpeted, and the rasping sound again—keys, poised and dangling from someone's hand? Roy? Jessie? *Jessie—*

Scream again, Jessie. Helll—

And someone running swiftly, light as a final sigh in winged sneakers; running down the darkness.

It is still hard to imagine Jessie Waterman lying there deciding—should she play dead, like a pet bitch, or play God, carrying the master's power of life and death in her mouth. Or were they the same? God, the irony of it. You would really have to know Jessie—the *old* Jessie—to appreciate the irony. She was the only girl in her college dormitory who was afraid of both cars and menstrual tampons. In her mid-thirties she still hadn't learned to drive; no one knew if she had conquered the other problem, but it was doubtful.

She was the kind of woman you hate to be with in a restaurant; she stared at the menu as if it were a final exam she was destined to fail. "Umm, that sounds . . . oh, no, wait. What's that they're having at the next table? I think . . . no, wait, does it have a sauce? What's in the sauce? Oh, I don't know, Roy, you decide." *Crazy cunt*, Roy would mutter, and order for her.

It must have been just after their second or third break-in that the Watermans began to talk seriously about moving. It was a standard joke among their friends who had fled years before that Roy and Jessie would never get out alive; that they seemed to be waiting purposely until after the Red Sea closed up again, out of some dark urge to be swallowed alive.

At parties they would huddle in corners swapping endless survival stories with other "lucky" victims of burglary or street crime. "Lucky" I wasn't home when they came; "lucky" they only took my money/roughed me up/hurt my child a little. They were forever compiling lists of loss for insurance adjusters, writing embarrassing letters to distant relatives asking, "Do you remember the little silver cup you gave us when Robin was born? If by any chance you still have the bill . . ."

And each time, they would pick up the strewn papers, bits of splintered furniture, shards of glass, murmuring that it didn't seem quite so bad as last time. "Lucky"—at least "this one" hadn't slashed the sofa or defecated on the rug.

They had a neighbor who boasted when his door was hacked to pieces with crowbars; it proved his lock was pickproof. They also knew a woman who had met "her" burglar on the street. She knew he was "hers" by his clothes—all of which had been stolen at various times from her husband's closet. "What happened when you recognized him?" Jessie asked, fascinated. "Oh, he recognized me, too," the woman said. "We nodded, like old friends. His nod meant 'Turn me in and I'll be back to kill you.' My nod meant 'I know.'" The woman shrugged. "It was a deal."

The Watermans had seemed satisfied with their deal, too. They were still alive. But then, right after that last big break-in, it stopped being enough. There's no telling what clinched it—maybe the children. One of Roy's daughters from the second marriage, kind of a sallow, nervous kid, had come to live with them, and then their little girl Robin started having bad dreams. She was almost nine then, all the baby fears still intact, and the grown-up ones crowding in on top. "Why do we stay here?" she kept asking them. She had one dream about a giant mechanical diamond cutting a perfect round manhole in the window, without making a sound. And another one about a helicopter landing on the roof. Grown-ups kept trying to laugh it off with her, of course; if burglars had diamonds or helicopters, they wouldn't have to break in. Robin thought that might be true for the diamond, but why couldn't they borrow a helicopter from a rich friend?

"Well," Jessie said, "wouldn't the rich friend just give them money?" And Robin explained, "Because he's mean about money. The only thing he doesn't mind sharing is his helicopter."

Then again, it might have been something else, nothing to do with the children at all, that made the Watermans decide to go. Maybe Jessie was the one who gave up. Jessie always quit things abruptly. She was living with a photographer, a man she'd been with over a year, when she walked out one night—without a suitcase—and married Roy Waterman. In those days young models—even very successful young models like Jessie—had a habit of suddenly marrying men like Roy Waterman. A producer of animated films for television, he was about twice her age and excessively married, with an alarming number of "ex-children," as he called them, scattered here and there with their mothers like so many pilot projects that had failed to generate sponsor interest.

Many people seemed shocked by Roy's casual breeding habits, and others were impressed that any man could owe so much child support, let alone pay it. It took a while to understand that Roy was neither embarrassed nor overwhelmed by his record, but simply pleased by what he regarded as a healthy male's creative output. He was only half joking when he said that he had never left a woman without at least impregnating her goodbye. The day he met Jessie, he predicted that she would be his next and best wife. His next and best—not his last.

Years later, when he was nearly fifty and Jessie was pregnant with their second child (his twelfth, or possibly thirteenth—he claimed to have lost count), Roy was still only half joking. "All my friends," he would sigh peevishly, "will be home in bed having nice, peaceful coronaries. I'll have mine pacing the goddamn maternity ward."

As it turned out, Jessie lost both the second baby and the third. Right after that she quit modeling, though she was still flagrantly beautiful. An intense four-color animated cartoon kind of beauty—thick mass of chrome-yellow hair, blue-black eyes (Waterman's ink). Her clothes had to be almost drab, black or white, and cut as severely as school uniforms, to tone her down. People gasped all the same; there was simply no other way to react to such a face. Her body hadn't changed either; it was still eight to twelve pounds too wholesome for the very-highest-fashion photographs. She was damned, she always said, if she'd ever give up sausage or thick bread or German potato salad for a lousy $100 an hour: "I'd rather starve." It was funny when she said it.

Indestructible. But she had a genuine horror of turning into an "old model," posing (at minimum rates) for ads in medical magazines. "Old models," most of them still beautiful and not old at all, were always photographed in dowdy clothes, in doctors' offices or filthy kitchens, wearing pained expressions indicating that once the magic has gone out of dishes and floor wax, only an extra-strength mood elevator can put it back. It was such a short drop, Jessie always said, from a Vogue cover to a clinically significant depression. And God knew the one had never been ruled out as a cause of the other.

Actually, all of that was an elaborate alibi. Jessie had wanted to quit modeling almost from the day she began. She considered it a cross between unskilled whoring and sleep-walking in a zoo—with the worst features of both. If only she hadn't made it so big. If only she hadn't married a man with too many children to support. But she had. So every morning, after putting on the day's face for the day's fortune, Jessie would stare at it in the mirror and burst into helpless tears. It wasn't the mirror image that made her so unhappy; it was just the reminder that her life depended on it.

Roy always knew how she felt, of course; and though he kept saying she could quit any time, they'd manage somehow, neither of them really thought that was true. And on some level, Jessie must have suspected, Roy liked the fact that she was a model. In a way it was the best damn career any wife of his could have had. The money, yes, but also the fact that no matter how much she made, it would never pose the slightest threat to the ego of a moderately successful film producer. A *model*, after all.

In any case, Jessie never cried for very long, those mornings. In spite of everything, she was thoroughly professional—and her eye makeup had already been applied.

Still, it was no surprise when, some months after the second miscarriage, Jessie told her agency no more bookings "for a while." And the next thing anyone heard was that the Watermans, of all people, were leaving. They had rented a house for the winter, way out at the bitterest end of Andrea Island —the last resort.

They had tried the area before, summers; the requisite spectacular waterscape, the small glassy house on a high rocky point, surrounded by empty sea and sky. In summer the isolation resembled simple breathing space—boats on the water and the voices of children wafting on black puffs of charcoal smoke from the sun decks of unseen neighbors a mile away.

Then last winter, on a crazy impulse, they had driven out one weekend in a snowstorm—three and a half hours—just to look at the place naked. And they fell in love with it that way, because of the silence.

Roy was the only one with doubts, at first. He still had to be at his office four and a half days a week. Commute by seaplane or helicopter, or stay in town and come out only for weekends, which meant leaving Jessie out there with the two girls. Robin wouldn't be a problem, but Diane surely would. Diane—Roy's sullen thirteen-year-old, who had come with some of the others for part of her summer vacation and then begged to stay. Her mother, Roy's second ex-wife, had remarried and was moving to California with her brood and two new stepchildren. One less was certainly okay with her. But out on some waterlogged cliff?

The local school was miles from the house; the bus would have to take a special detour to pick them up. Jessie still couldn't drive, and what if there were emergencies?

Ah, but the silence. The peace. Out there, even in the summer, a hood ornament stolen off a car parked on Main Street made page one with a two-column headline.

Out there the stare of a stranger was not an explosive device. Children's bicycles were not shackled with heavy chains. And at night, people who walked along quiet roads did not flinch at shadows.

"I'll take driving lessons," Jessie promised, knowing she wouldn't. "I'll read feminist tracts." (She wouldn't.) "I'll make poems or an herb garden. Banana bread. A quilt. Terra-cotta fertility masks." None of the above. She was not, after all, a new woman, but an "old" woman in a new time. Her marriage was old, like her husband and her fears. Yet there was something, had been something, askew all along. A sense of displacement, or of never having been placed. It was stirring now.

"I'll play with Robin and Diane, and we'll tell secrets about what we want to be unless we grow up."

Of course it was a reckless scheme; but then, whose life style was not a reckless scheme any more? So it was arranged. They sublet their upper-half-brownstone apartment, and forfeited $300 in private school registration fees, and sent careful reassurances to Diane's mother, who was easily reassured. Waterlogged cliff? Fine.

Roy began flying into town every Monday, and staying till Friday in the small West Side walk-up of a friend who was away making films in Europe. There was even room for Jessie, if she ever wanted to come in, say, on a Tuesday and stay overnight, arrange for the girls to stay with friends "out there." Maybe she'd do that, she said. (She wouldn't.)

Miraculous, the way the pieces all fell into place. The excitement of Roy's brave little journeys—tiny silvery plane gleaming like a toy over the gray morning tide, floating in and out of the real world. Jessie standing high on the point, scanning the distance between them with shaded eyes, like an ancient mariner's wife. Reading shapes in the mist as if they were tea leaves. Roy would vanish and Roy would reappear, and in between she had her life.

Every Monday after the plane took off and the bus came to collect the two girls, Jessie would celebrate her freedom by rushing out to the tall beach grass, clutching handfuls of stale bread, rotten lettuce, containers filled with mysterious gray furry-coated sauces, and hurling it all into the sea. Roy was a garbage inspector; Roy could not stand it when food spoiled, or when she used new vegetables, shoving the old ones back into the dim recesses of the refrigerator. Roy would open the garbage before throwing it away, and fish out the wilted lettuce leaf. "Why didn't you use it before it went bad?" he would say, reasonably. Roy was a speck on the horizon; Jessie smiled, tossing dead radishes over the cliff.

Sometimes she would open the refrigerator and stand there gulping draughts of icy air like pure oxygen, with the dreamy look of a vain woman on the threshold of a walk-in closet. Dazed by the gleam of sequins, the shimmer of satin, the marabou feathers trembling when she sighed. Beautiful. "Shut the refrigerator door," Roy would say, sensibly. No. She would stand there forever, reaching greedily inside, tearing at bread and cheese with her bare hands, scooping peanut butter from the jar with her perfect oval fingernails. Blissful; disgusting. "You would punish the children for what you're doing," Roy would say. Perhaps.

Later she would fall asleep sprawled in chairs, on floors, with her feet on the furniture. "Honey, look at the soles of your feet!" (Roy.) Ten in the morning, two in the afternoon, sometimes minutes after breakfast, her head on the table amid the cereal bowls. Often she would sleep half the day, waking groggily minutes before the bus was due; just in time to splash water at her eyes, so the children would think she had been doing whatever regular mothers do.

Oh, she would cook and clean, fitfully. Especially clean. Especially in fits. She would look into a mirror and see no Jessie, only the house. Chairs coated with cat hairs and dust, floors littered with clothes and magazines, corners blurred with cobwebs, windows etched with salt spray. The house, clean, was her only shield; her talisman. Clean, it would catch the pale sun and keep her safe. Otherwise she was lost. Monday to Friday she would submit to the house—as if it were Roy.

Incredible, how she had hungered for that solitude, her separate peace. The lifting of Roy's crushing weight, the release from the agency, the bookings, the city, the fear—all it had freed her for was this: wiping at surfaces; wasting food; licking her fingers; sleeping, sleeping.

But at night she lay awake nursing her secret, which grew inside her like a tumor or a monstrous child: hating Roy, hating Jessie. She felt it constantly, an oceanic current pulling at her, stretching and tearing from within. Sometimes the pressure made her weak; she would sink to the bed in a near-faint, or run out of the house, gasping for air, to climb a high rock and lie there outstretched like a captive seal, bleating and panting. Still the feeling pulled at her womb, churning. Often she would sit or stand very still, listening for signs of its life. She studied the effect it had on her breathing, on her

24

silhouette against the dark bedroom wall, in the rise and fall of her voice when she spoke his name aloud.

But when she studied her face in the mirror she thought only about Jessie. What was happening to Jessie. Only a corner of my space now, a tiny corner. That's all she takes, Jessie thought. No more than Roy, but no less. Safely encapsulated, the two of them. Fraternal twins. Sometimes Jessie felt them both at once, pressing against her, squeezing, fighting for her air. The one she thought of as *her* was more dangerous. She was quieter, but Jessie understood why—she was rooted, attached like a vestigial organ. Of no further use, yet still full of life. Demanding nourishment and sapping Jessie's strength, capable of infecting her, subjecting her to wounds of various kinds. She could— Jessie thought she might— What if she puffed up like a venomous toad and burst? Jessie would shudder and move away from the mirror, lest it read her thoughts. Nonsense. Must find a way to control this, she would tell herself firmly. Tear her out somehow. Tear her. . . .

Chapter 2

EVERYONE PREDICTED that Roy would be happy once they moved—amazingly happy. And he was. He exulted, like a powerful man celebrating his release from a confined space. He was less in control of his world, but he was also free— and freedom was distracting.

Even in the commuting, Roy seemed to find an element of magic and celebration. His spirits would lift each time the little plane pierced a cloud or tilted rakishly toward the sun. Below him the bay and sea shimmered like dark banquet cloths set with crystal.

Roy had always been a nature lover. It was his saving grace, that violent physical responsiveness he had to the kind of natural beauty that could not be manipulated, least of all by him. He managed to keep this aspect of his personality well hidden, since in his profession it would have marked him as a vulnerable man, a man of insufficient hardness. Which would not have been fair at all.

Roy respected hardness. Indeed, he had chosen to live by it, insofar as he had a choice. He had a hard edginess. He drove hard bargains. He believed in the hard sell, and his achievements were hard-won. Nevertheless he hungered privately for color and pure space, open sea and sky, clear blues and honest grays. And he kept his weakness for beauty to himself so that he could move as murderously well as a man had to move, in essentially ugly territory. He kept a gun now, under his pillow. That was something he could talk about.

Jessie, of course, answered both of Roy's instinctive needs. Being beautiful, she satisfied his inordinate longing for perfection in the natural order of things. Being his wife, she confirmed his manly power. Other men envied him. That too was beautiful. And that too was natural. It was somewhat more difficult to guess which side of Roy had appealed to Jessie instinctively. Jessie herself thought it was the tender heart of the beast she loved, but it was clearly the beastly exterior she had married. And as the marriage had aged, Roy's soft core had seemed to atrophy from lack of use. Or perhaps the hardness had metastasized inside him because a man constantly needed more of it in reserve, to draw on, just to get along. In any case, Jessie scarcely remembered the tenderness any more—only that it had been there.

But Roy's esthetic pulse did seem to quicken with the new life; his eyes were bright, and there was pleasure in his quiet voice when he described his island, his house, his flying. He said he had a sense of "rightness" in his life—for the first time since he had met Jessie. The joy began to evaporate, however, as Jessie's loneliness—or what he took to be her loneliness— began to gnaw at him. At first he thought he knew what was wrong. "She may not make it out there," he would say cautiously to their city friends. "It's too rough on a woman, isolation." To a few, he confided, with a laugh to take the edge off, "She's miserable. I should have known you can't let a woman go all week without fucking. They dry up and blow away. I should give her another baby."

27

Some of the friends who kept in touch with Jessie regularly, by letter or telephone, tried to reassure him. "She says it's okay. She says it's beautiful."

"*It* is," Roy snapped. "*She's* not."

On week nights when he called her from the city, the new chill was always in her voice. It lingered, even in her silences. And on weekends when he was with her, the emptiness between them acquired a threnodic rhythm, like the hum of unknown creatures in the dark. He would command her to talk to him. "What *is* it?" he would demand. She would rouse herself, with a slight frown. Recognition would flash across her eyes like pain, as if she had been struggling to recall his name. "Yes," she would say absently, and then come over and kneel on the floor in front of him, to be stroked or fondled. Sometimes she would suck him, kneeling, but even then he felt only her body serving his. Blind reflex. She was somewhere else. He shuddered. Jessie. His Jessie. "Stop it," he would groan finally. "What?" she would say. "Talk to me." She would blink, uncomprehending, as if he had roused her from sleep. "But I did talk, Roy. Before—didn't I?"

Kneeling there she would be thinking Phallus. This is the real one, not the gun. So hard to remember. Everything they make to remind you—buildings, cars, bombs, crucifixes. All weapons that control or hurt. Leave them with you when they're gone, for safekeeping. For keeping you safe, in your place. They'll be back. Even the words, enough to make you remember. They'll be back. Even the words, enough to make you remember. Thrust, drive, penetrate, shoot. Things you shouldn't, never learned how, think you can't. Wouldn't dare. Or if you try, it's funny. You imitating. Phallic woman. What you need. . . .

But look at the real one. Roy's is real. Feel it. Taste. . . . Soft, vulnerable. Nothing like a gun, really. Nothing like the words. Buildings, guns, words. Blown up out of proportion, so you forget how soft, how vulnerable. Think phallus is a monster, destroyer. See it in the movie ads. Long, black, loaded, aiming at you. Fire when ready. Always ready. They never show the real one—can't. You'd notice the actual size, softness, limited striking power. When they do want to show a real one, they find a monster. Shock of seeing it enlarges it in your mind. They count on that.

Don't know if there are any real ones any more. Maybe they're all guns. Guns are more . . . reliable.

"What are you thinking?" Roy would ask.

"About you," she would say. "About this."

He spoke about these strange silences of hers. Occasionally, and with careful nonchalance, to old friends, most of whom found it hard to believe. Everyone who had worked with Jessie in her modeling days knew her as golden—but never silent. "Believe," Roy said to them all, darkly. "Dead silent."

Well, he could have been exaggerating. Just as he had, during his very first week in town alone, about waking in the night wracked with intense physical pain. Body hunger, he said, for Jessie. The kind of complaining husbands often do when they are making the necessary adjustments to a temporary single life. In Roy's case it seemed just a routine bid for sexual attention. There were, after all, a number of available bodies that could be pressed into service. Kate Saville's, for instance.

Kate—Jessie's old college chum and onetime roommate—was freshly divorced at the time, and handy, since she was doing advertising art work for a studio in Roy's office building. It was logical that they should meet now and then in the elevator, at the lobby newsstand, in nearby coffee shops, in bed. The world they inhabited had always been full of institutions. Midday martinis were one; afternoon naps at convenient apartments and hotel rooms were another. Something that everyone had, and nobody really counted, except perhaps as a business expense.

Even before her friend Jessie married him, Kate had been acutely aware of the negative pull Roy exerted on women.

His apparent contempt for them, which he flaunted like a campaign button, was magnetic. There were women who denied that this was the basis for their attraction. They insisted that, "underneath," Roy wasn't like that at all. It was true, in a way, but not in a way that he ever exposed to casual female acquaintances. It was almost a comedy routine for him to talk to a woman in public without taking his eyes off her breasts, or his hands off some other sexual part, so that either she forgot what she was saying, or everyone else did. If the woman objected, he might apologize, but often with a sly little grin, and then a helpless shrug. "But what do you expect," he would sigh, "when you look"—and he would look, again—"like that?"

The fact was that Roy was no more of a sexual bully than most men of his time and place. He tended to bully women who liked or expected it, and those who could tell—even without seeing the evidence—that "underneath" lurked a soft, and probably hurt, little boy, crying for a mother's love. God knew they were right—Jessie mothered him, just as he fathered her.

There were other women, though, like Kate Saville, who defended themselves against Roy's appeal by laughing uncomfortably at him, or marveling aloud at his stubborn refusal to change his style, long after it had become embarrassing. One of the last great dinosaurs, she called him—a relic from the golden age of misogyny. Womanizing was no longer the sport of kings, or so she had heard; the kings were supposed to be dead. But for Kate, and probably for most of the others, the discomfort was still more genuine than the brave new laughter. There was still a yielding part of them—somewhere behind the knees, between the thighs, or deep inside the womb—that drew them to Roy Waterman in spite of themselves. He would say "cunt" in that impossible tone that made it sound like an insolent caress. And even as they despised him for it, even as their eyes blazed, that other part, wherever it was, still answered, Yes—oh, yes.

It was considered somewhat remarkable that Kate had spent so many years neatly sidestepping the obligatory affair with Roy. Most people ascribed it—mistakenly—to either her superior powers of resistance or her quaint sense of old-fashioned loyalty to Jessie. But the credit, if it was credit, belonged entirely to Roy, who had always considered it faintly incestuous, and therefore open to criticism, to seduce one's wife's closest friend.

What changed his mind was Kate. She was fairly subtle about it, in the sense that what finally happened between her and Roy seemed to grow naturally out of her passionate solicitousness for Jessie during the Watermans' critical transition period. It was Kate who, almost single-handed (to hear her tell it), planned and executed every detail of their move to the island. She helped them pack, helped set up the borrowed apartment Roy was to occupy, even filled in the duplicate kitchen necessities for his new bachelor life—the single-egg poacher, the one-cup espresso maker, the serrated knife for his morning grapefruit. She thought of everything. "Poor Jessie," she told everyone, whether they asked or not. "She's so upset, so *crazy*, she can't handle any of these things. I have to do it all." Of course Kate paid for everything out of her own pocket; of course she never allowed the Watermans to reimburse her; and of course when she told all their mutual friends how helpful she had been, she said they had *sent* her all over town on these nuisance errands, and never even offered to pay her back. "Oh, well," she would sigh, "I guess that's what friendship is all about—exploitation." She would shake her head, like a doctor who has done everything possible, and now it's in Someone Else's hands. And so, while Jessie—according to Kate—wept helplessly into her packing crates, Kate began shepherding the Waterman children all over town—to museums and shops, to movies, zoos, Gilbert and Sullivan revivals. She was exhausted. "I have no life of my own," she would sigh. But if anyone dared suggest that she didn't really have to adopt Jessie's life—or Jessie's children

31

—her eyes would blaze with righteous piety. "Jessie *needs* me," she would say.

The truth was that Kate's solicitude made Jessie acutely uncomfortable. "I wish you wouldn't. . . ." she would protest. "We *can* manage."

"Oh, please," Kate would cry, devastated. "I'm not doing it for you—it's for me! Purely selfish." Her soft dark eyes would quiver with genuine hurt. "Please let me." And so, reluctantly, Jessie would let her do too much. Later, of course, Kate would tell anyone who would listen exactly how much that was. The errands, the chores, the circus tickets, the expensive, worthless souvenirs ("But Robin wanted it so! The poor little thing!"). And somehow it would seem as though Jessie had forced her to give herself, her time, her money. "I asked for it," Kate would say, with a martyred shrug. "I get carried away, loving people."

She left little doubt in anyone's mind that Jessie took shocking advantage of her. "But she can't help it," Kate would add, in the tone of one who knows dark secrets. "Imagine being married to a Roy Waterman. Imagine being his *child.*"

If anyone ever pressed her for details—did Roy *beat* the children? Was Jessie having a *breakdown?*—Kate would shake her head sorrowfully, as though she couldn't possibly tell the worst of it.

And so Kate served all the functions of a lively gossip columnist, a moralistic confession magazine, and a brilliant troublemaker. She entertained everyone's worst instincts—like a clever child whose malicious mischief passes for fun. Still, most of her friends eventually found her trying. She demanded too much attention. Clinging to other people's lives—lives she considered more lustrous than her own—like a drowning victim, and then kicking and thrashing to deny that they were merely letting her hang on. She professed utter devotion and utter contempt—for the same people, at the same time. And she almost always got away with it, for a little while. Showering everyone with her poisonous favors.

Telephoning constantly; sending flowers and small, thoughtful gifts; confessing her own most shameful flaws so that others would be disarmed and tell her theirs. She collected people's fears, sins, sexual ineptitudes, failures and misfortunes, and crawled inside them for as long as she was allowed to stay. It was a living.

After Jessie and the girls were gone, Kate came back to their apartment to continue doing whatever she could—water the plants, check on the mail, take the forgotten library books back and pay the fines. She cooked things and carried them across town to Roy's new "pied-à-terre," and explained that "Jessie begged me to—she said he was starving."

By then it was clear that the Watermans could not exist without Kate Saville. It seemed only natural that she should go on being indispensable to Roy, as if Jessie had personally appointed her. "I don't know how to get out of it now," she would sigh. "I'm the maid."

Still, no one who knew them suspected that what she might have been after, during all of this, was Roy. She had never before evinced any special craving for forbidden fruit; the thought that, in "borrowing" Roy when Jessie wasn't using him, she might actually be risking her friendship with Jessie scarcely occurred to her. If anything, her encounter with Roy —which sputtered on and off over several months—seemed to be a device for bringing her closer to Jessie than ever. It was apparent to everyone they knew that the absent Jessie seemed to grow more beautiful, more fascinating and more valuable to Kate, the more bitterly Roy complained about her coldness, her withdrawal, her failure as his wife.

It was as though Kate never thought she was taking anything away from Jessie, nor even sharing anything secretly with her. She actually seemed to be reaching—or being carried—closer to Jessie through Roy. Kate herself never really understood what she was doing, but that was how it worked out.

Besides, the two women had been friends for so long,

through so many genuine crises—from college to the first days of Jessie's marriage and the last days of Kate's—that it looked as if nothing could ever disconnect them. They had traded so many secrets, and articles of clothing, that neither could be sure exactly what had first belonged to whom. It didn't matter. They had cheated together on exams, and covered for each other, and talked each other out of suicide, and shared the last soggy Kleenex after crying all night. Jessie was the person Kate had called at three A.M. when her marriage broke up. Kate was the one Jessie had called when she lost her babies, and when she suspected the first of Roy's infidelities, and when she stopped caring how many there were. By now the two women even seemed to resemble each other, despite the difference in their size and coloring. Kate was a smaller, darker and more fragile version of Jessie. Both the resemblance and the difference lay primarily in the way they smiled —a certain light filling Jessie's face from within, and the same light flashing across Kate's like an applied cosmetic.

All things considered, it appeared to be a very safe bet that Kate Saville's sleeping with Roy Waterman would have very little to do with Kate and Jessie's friendship. At the same time, however, Kate also sensed that sleeping with Roy would connect her to Jessie in a new and very important way, possibly the most important way, now that Jessie herself was out of reach.

Roy never worried about the consequences of his affair with Kate, either. He seemed not to take it seriously, once it began, though he did make it plain that he thought it would be nice if Kate didn't "report" to Jessie quite so often, while it was going on. He also found it disconcerting, he said, that Jessie had an uncanny way of calling Kate every time he happened to be in Kate's bed—and that Kate never seemed in any hurry to hang up. "Why don't you talk to her on your own time?" he complained once. "This is my own time," Kate replied.

For a while he was disconcerted enough to drop out of

Kate's sex life altogether. He was involved briefly with Maria Folliott, the sculptor, though that was an unlikely combination, even briefly. Maria did massive male nudes in dark wood and leather. They exuded a raw, sinister power, and so, apparently, did she. Within a few weeks she had given Roy up for one of her dark leather men, and he went back to Kate Saville. This time Kate realized—long before Roy did—why he was there. He needed someone who would remind him of Jessie, even while taking his mind off her. Kate was the inevitable choice.

"You know," he said to her that first night of their renewed partnership, "I don't trust you worth a damn."

"I know," Kate said, playfully. "You consider me dangerous. You think I'd tell Jessie anything."

"Wouldn't you?"

"Sure. I never lie to a friend."

"Would you lie *for* her—to protect her?"

She hesitated. "No," she said gravely, piously. "Jessie'd hate me to do that."

Roy laughed. "Come here," he said, "and show me exactly what Jessie'd hate."

Kate rose delightedly to the occasion. And from then on, whenever Jessie called at an inopportune moment, Roy took great pains not to let it interrupt him. "You just talk . . . as long as you like," he would tell Kate, smiling. "I'll be doing . . . whatever I'd be doing . . . anyway."

Kate never did tell Jessie about that. She found her new role in their life much too exciting to spoil it. It would be no exaggeration to say that she was very much in love with that role. More than she ever was with Roy.

And things continued to deteriorate between Roy and Jessie. He talked about it constantly now, sifting the evidence of her unhappiness, searching for clues, finding nothing. Every weekend she spent hour after hour in the same room with him, reading or sketching or playing some word game with the children. She never spoke to him except for monosyllabic replies to direct questions. Sometimes she would disappear into the kitchen, or the bedroom, or out of the house to walk along the narrow rocky beach—and never say where she was going, or for how long, or would he like to come too. She never complained; she never explained. If he asked, if he probed, she looked puzzled or she looked away.

It had never been like this between them. They had always talked endlessly, recklessly, to each other. When Jessie was modeling, even on extended location trips to Europe, Hawaii, Japan, she could never wait to sort out her impressions of what was happening to her before calling him, letting her thoughts tumble out across the distance between them like gifts she had not had time to wrap.

And now the silence was her only gift. She never acknowledged that it came from her. He was a helpless irritant in her house, a pebble of sand trapped under her smooth shell. Witnessing her pain—for it must be pain, he thought—but powerless to relieve it, he wanted her at least to cover him with some lovely nacreous substance of herself, to seal him inside and protect them both and make them forever valuable to each other. But she exuded no healing balm; she only withdrew still further from him—he could feel her recoiling —and vanished within some other part of her shell, to lick her wound as if it were a secret lover.

"Talk to me," he still begged her.

"Again?" she would sigh gently, turning her smile on low, like a sunlamp. And patiently she would repeat the neutral things she had already said to him. "I asked you what you wanted for dinner, and I told you we needed milk—I mentioned that Diane locked herself in her room again last night, and that Robin got an A on her spelling test, and that neither of them has any friends. . . ."

Halfway through her recital, he would explode; accuse her of provoking him; revile her. And she would wind her silence more securely around her. Eventually, mercifully, the weekend would end.

Chapter 3

SOMETIMES ROY FELT RESIGNED to the change in Jessie. Maybe there was nothing he could do; maybe she was merely going mad out there all alone. Most women probably would. Perhaps the move had simply been a mistake after all. And since Jessie had been the one who really wanted it, maybe she couldn't admit how serious a mistake. Next year they could move back to town.

He did not stop urging her to come in with him for a day or two. He knew it would help for her to see her friends, shop, cover the galleries. She should touch base with . . . reality. She smiled at that. Maybe she would come in with him sometime. Meaning no.

Yet whenever Kate called Jessie, to say hello or how much she missed her, Jessie invariably sounded her usual serene self. Wry, of course. Quieter, maybe—but even that could have been the distance, or the connection. Or the fact that her voice, without that golden face around it, transmitted only a pale shadow of Jessieness. "It's so dead here," she said lightly. "I feel like Persephone, except I can't even get pomegranates. They're out of season." Kate said she could probably send her a box from some exotic underworld greengrocer, and Jessie laughed. "They'd cost four dollars apiece, and Roy would never let me spit out the seeds."

Jessie also joked about Diane, the thirteen-year-old, commemorating her father's weekly visits by putting on four pounds while he was there. It was an improvement—she used to gain six. Except for school, Diane was sleeping most of the day and eating most of the night. She also masturbated excessively, often in front of people, and occasionally even in class. Jessie thought she had cut down on the masturbating, though—or else she had found a quieter way of doing it. Either way, Jessie said, the sea air was having its effect.

Though they often talked about nothing much for half an hour or more, Jessie never seemed to prolong the call out of boredom or loneliness. In fact, it was usually Kate who placed the call, and it was always Jessie who had to hang up first. (Of course Kate told everyone else that it was Jessie who made the calls; who clung to the telephone for dear life; who found life empty without Kate Saville.)

So although Kate never openly challenged Roy's dark portrait of Jessie as a seasick Emily Brontë, brooding alone on the windswept rocks, she had never really heard a trace of it in Jessie's voice.

And then one night Jessie paused in midsentence—something about Roy planning a long business trip to Europe—and blurted, almost inaudibly, "Listen, Kate, could you possibly come out and stay with me awhile? I . . . need you."

"Oh, sure," Kate said, too light and quick, because she was acutely uncomfortable.

"When?" Jessie pressed her.

"Well, when do you—"

"Now." But now Jessie was laughing, so that it might all have been a joke, except it definitely wasn't.

"Well," Kate said, "how about next week? I could—"

"Roy will be gone," Jessie said, not indicating whether that was good or bad. Kate realized that Jessie hadn't said a word to Roy about inviting her. She couldn't quite bring herself to mention it, even jokingly.

"Well," Kate said again, stalling now. She could hear Jessie breathing; she could tell Jessie wasn't sure she could work this out.

"Look," said Jessie finally, trying to sound breezy and casual, "why don't I check everyone's schedule, and we'll see . . . what makes sense."

"Fine," said Kate. "Any time's good for me."

Kate knew that Roy would be angry with her; she guessed he would also be angry with Jessie. But would he try to stop the visit? On what pretext? It had been a long time since Kate had given any thought to the odd shape of their triangle.

Within five minutes, Roy had dialed Kate's number and forbidden her to go. He did not shout; he was merely icy, masterful and terrifyingly calm.

"You're not going," he said, without so much as hello. "I don't know what made you say you were, but you're not. Is that clear?"

Kate drew a deep breath. She had spent a lot of time telling herself that she was not afraid of Roy Waterman. "Roy, listen—"

"Shut up," he said. She did. "Now," he said, "you listen, bitch. I can't stop you from confessing your sins to my wife on the telephone—but I can certainly stop you from invading my house in order to expose mine."

"It's Jessie's house, too," Kate whimpered.

"I, don't, want, you, there." He snapped off the words like crisp bills.

Kate tried to control the whine in her voice, but she could hear it.

"*Jessie* wants me there," she said. "Doesn't that count?"

39

"Jessie," he said, "is *my* problem."

"I don't think she would define herself that way." (That was good, she thought, I got him with that.)

"I'm warning you, Kate—"

"No, you're not," she said, suddenly feeling brave and reckless. "Jessie has no idea that I've ever touched your lovely naked body, and I'm not about to tell her any of your filthy secrets. Not even if she pulls out my fingernails, one by one. So what are you afraid of? She's dying of loneliness, and you're going away, and all I'm doing is going out to visit an old friend—because she asked me to. *I* didn't ask *her!"* Damn it, she thought, I'm crying.

"Your friend," he said coldly. "Some friend."

"Oh, what the hell is that supposed to mean?" she sobbed.

"It means," he said, all calm again, "that you're not going, damn you. Call her up and make some excuse, that's all. Some very plausible excuse. I'm sure you'll think of a beaut."

He hung up. Kate's hands were shaking. "Look at that," she said. But she didn't call Jessie back. She never knew what, if anything, Roy ever said to Jessie about the visit, but the next day Jessie called again to make sure Kate was coming, and Kate agreed to fly out there the following Monday, the day after Roy was to leave.

Unfortunately his trip was delayed a day, and Jessie didn't see why Kate shouldn't come ahead as scheduled. Kate had not heard another word from Roy all week, and she refused to worry about the awkwardness of being out there with him. Serves him right, she thought. That was a mistake, but she was too angry to see it.

By the time Kate arrived, it had become clear that she should have seen it—and given Roy a chance to get away. Jessie had been crying; the tension in the house was palpable. "I probably shouldn't have come," Kate said uncomfortably, as Jessie led her to the guest room. "Roy is furious."

Jessie smiled, except for her eyes. "I needed you to come,"

she said. "Anyway, Roy is always furious. That's how he lets us know he's home."

Kate watched her friend moving absently from linen closets to bathrooms, collecting towels, forgetting to put them down. They moved to the kitchen—she was still carrying the towels. Finally Jessie stopped abruptly to stare at the bundle in her arms, mystified. She seemed fragmented, disoriented—as though she might have suffered a slight accident and been skillfully restored, almost as good as new. Kate thought of a lovely Victorian glass painting her family had once owned, one of those jewel-colored floral bouquets against a black ground, all painted on the back of an oval glass. Someone had opened a champagne bottle in the room where it hung, and the plastic cork had flown wild, hitting it. Though the glass was held together securely by the heavy gold frame, the damage was irreparable—a delicate cobweb of crazing across the face of the painting. It was barely discernible. The light had to catch it in a certain way, and even then you had to stand very close to notice it, unless you knew how it had been before.

In the living room, Roy sulked behind a newspaper, radiating quills of pointed silence. Only once did he speak directly to Kate, when Jessie was out of the room. "You'll regret this; I swear you will."

"I already regret it," Kate murmured. "I did try to change it, you know. To come tomorrow. But Jessie insisted."

"You could have handled it," he said tersely. "It's not as though she were ill."

"Yes it is," Kate retorted. "Needing is a kind of ill. And loneliness is. But never mind. I'm sorry you're so angry. I—won't stay long."

"The hell you won't," he said dryly, raising the paper higher to ward her off.

The house was lovely, all green and white and glass, with enormous botanical illustrations hung along the walls in thin silver frames—anatomy of a pear blossom and its fruit; of an apple, a peach. Sensual but wholesome—like Jessie. Kate smiled.

There were also countless photographs of Jessie all over the house. Hung on walls and massed together on tables. Framed in silver, in gold, in mosaic, in lucite. Jessie in black and white wearing enigmatic smiles, quizzical frowns, seductive winks. Jessie in color laughing with her head thrown back. Standing with her feet apart. Running away from home. Motorcycling. Motorcycling? *Jessie?* Swaddled in fur, in silk chiffon, in leather like a Hell's Angel. Playing in water. Emerging from pools, rainstorms, bathtubs, oceans. Jessie immersed in bubbles, in foam, in mist. Jessie's hair streaming over her shoulders like molten gold. Her eyelashes in tiny wet clumps, glistening. You could almost taste the salt on them.

Jessie and the two girls fluttered around trying to appease Roy and play hostess to Kate, all at once. None of it worked. They baked a soufflé that fell and made a mess in the stove; Roy shouted at them. Diane and Robin fussed endlessly over the salad, squabbling over who could cut the radish into a more perfect tiny rose; Robin cut her finger; Roy shouted, banishing them both from the kitchen. Diane retreated to her room in tears, slamming the door. Robin would not stop crying. Kate cringed. Roy shouted.

Jessie brought him tea with rum and a sprig of fresh mint from her window herb garden. Roy let the tea grow cold without touching it. And finally the three adults sat stiffly, watching the rain through the glass window walls, worrying about whether Roy's plane would take off tomorrow, or whether they would have to endure it all through another whole day. They kept saying nothing for endless minutes, and then furiously talking at once—flinging desperate politenesses into the air, like sacrifices. "Can I get you—?" "Would anyone like—?" "Is it too cool in here?" "Shall we light a fire?"

At last the rain stopped, and Jessie asked Kate to come outside for a walk along the narrow beach. They walked in silence for a while, a sheltering silence. Jessie's thoughts embraced her friend like welcoming arms. They stood for a moment watching the soft grays of sky and water blend skillfully together, as in a charcoal drawing.

"I'm not unhappy here, you know," Jessie said. "I mean I can't imagine going back, ever. Roy keeps saying I should— for a day or two. Does he think I'm cracking up?"

"The tyranny of 'should,'" Kate sighed. "Even here!"

"Well, does he think that?" Jessie persisted.

"Cracking up? No, I don't think he thinks that. Unhappy though. Cut off. He's worried about you."

"Cut off!" Jessie laughed. "Like a shipwreck survivor in a cartoon? Hollow-eyed and ragged. Dripping and sexually starved. Building a raft out of strange feelings that will never carry me anywhere." She stopped smiling. "But of course they're all I have."

"What feelings?"

Jessie didn't answer, and they went on walking.

"When Roy comes," she began, after another long silence, "we put on a play. Robin and Diane and I. We all sit at the table like ladies in a nice family. The way we used to in the city. We eat without talking, as a rule—we always did that. Trying not to let the fork click against our teeth, or make noise drinking our water, or cry if Roy shouts. The only difference now is that Roy doesn't shout. He doesn't destroy the silence. He respects it now. It's mine." She paused and looked at Kate gravely. Kate said nothing.

"Funny, isn't it?" Jessie asked.

"What?"

"That dinner is the funeral. Every night the family celebrates its own death."

"What happens," Kate asked cautiously, "when Roy is away?"

43

"Oh," she said, "then we are all children; I'm one of them. We eat standing up, or running. Or in bed. Diane eats in bed. Sometimes I forget to eat. . . . Kate, do you suppose I'm always one of them? And only pretend to be a grown-up in front of him?"

"Are you afraid of Roy?" Kate asked.

"Aren't you?"

Now it was Kate who didn't answer. But she held Jessie's hand walking back to the house. She had never done that before.

At the door, Jessie said, "Wait; I have to tell you what it's like." She hesitated, as if she weren't sure how to go on. Kate said nothing. "It's like . . . giving up smoking," Jessie said finally. "You begin by cutting down to the ones you know you absolutely must have—the ones you can't live without. Like the ones after meals, that taste the best. And then after a few days you forget why you needed those so much; you taste each one carefully as though it's something new. And it is—strange and harsh. You see, you're not used to the harshness any more. And then, finally, one day you light one, the morning one, that you still remember needing most of all, all those years. And it makes you sick. You're . . . immune. That's it; that's how it is." Her eyes were full of tears.

Kate could not speak; she wanted only to touch Jessie at that moment, just touch her hair, or her face. Instead she let go of Jessie's hand, because her own hand felt as if it might burst into flame.

"Roy and I—" Kate blurted helplessly.

"Oh, ssh," Jessie said, and touched Kate's mouth with one finger. "I don't care."

"Neither do I," said Kate, and they both began to laugh. Crazily—like little girls laughing out of control, giggling over naughty secrets, over anything at all. Irrepressible, floating laughter like balloons caught by the wind. As if they had let go of the string, after being warned: Hold on, now, tight, whatever you do—don't let go.

44

The next day, after Roy left, the weather became unseasonably warm and muggy. Jessie changed from slacks into very short white shorts, and Kate found herself staring at Jessie— at her thighs, at the creases in the shorts, at the way they clung to Jessie's body. She wanted—no, she didn't. But what if she were to reach out, suddenly, and just hold her hand against Jessie's smooth, pale-gold thigh? Right then, while Jessie was talking about—about what? I'm sorry, Jessie, she thought, I wasn't—

So then Kate tried to keep her eyes on Jessie's face, but there was Jessie's mouth, and Kate could still feel Jessie's finger on her own mouth, where Jessie had touched it the night before. Jessie's throat, maybe—safe to look at a person's throat? It had, though, tiny golden hairs that gleamed when the sun caught them, and a little pulse beating at the center. Kate couldn't hear Jessie's words at all any more, watching that pulse throb. She imagined it fluttering like a bird's heartbeat, and she wanted, just one fingertip, just there—or, no, the tip of her tongue. She wanted—the tip, held to it like a match. Jessie would taste like . . . butterscotch? Exactly.

"What are you *thinking* about?" Jessie said.

Oh, God, Jessie, Kate thought, I'm thinking about tasting you. "I think I'm incredibly hungry," Kate said quickly, her eyes avoiding the blue light of Jessie's gaze.

"I never believed," Jessie murmured, "that sea air creates an appetite. A life maybe, but hardly an appetite."

Kate laughed. She had almost forgotten the specialness of Jessie. Quite apart from her physical perfection, she was a strange and wonderful creature, full of sudden discomforting insights and improbable passions. Jessie loved, with equivalent fervor, fresh strawberries, real pearls, anything vanilla, and the color violet—which she never wore because she never wore any color. She really belonged in some other, more elegant time. Or, rather, she pretended that this *was* such a time, regardless of realities that proved it couldn't be. When she spoke, when she smiled, it simply became the kind of world

45

she belonged in. Kate felt it again that day, the buoyant gaiety of Jessie's old spirit that had always made everything else seem somehow less real than Jessie.

Once Kate had called her late at night, and Jessie had asked why her voice sounded so funny. "Because I'm eating cheese," Kate had said. Most people would have said, "Oh," and let it go. Jessie was instantly captivated. "What kind of cheese?" she wanted to know. She *really* wanted to know. There was an appreciation of cheese in her voice. A knowledge of cheese. A delight.

Kate remembered another time, long ago, in college—when she and Jessie and another girl, Paulette, had been engrossed in a serious talk about sudden death. Being found in a street or a roadway, without identification, and having one's body examined by the authorities.

"The deceased woman," Kate had said, "appeared to be about nineteen years of age, and had capped teeth. A check of dental records revealed . . ."

Paulette, who was obsessed with being overweight, turned pale. "Do they *weigh* you?" she gasped. "I mean do they *publish* the weight?"

Jessie shut her eyes and intoned, "The torso alone . . ." and they had all, even Paulette, roared with laughter. Kate could still hear Jessie's lyrical, soft voice: "The torso *alone* . . ."

"You know anything about weapons, Kate?" Jessie was asking.

"Weapons?"

Jessie laughed. "You live alone on an island, you begin to think about funny things."

"Funny things," Kate echoed. "You mean like guns?"

"Not guns," said Jessie quickly, wincing. "Roy keeps one—" She bit her lip. "I've been thinking more about female weapons."

"Ah," said Kate. "Venus flytrap?"

Jessie ignored the joke. "Traps," she said, shaking her head, "only *look* female. Time bombs too, because they're hidden

46

in bushes, or locked in boxes. Makes you think of them lying in wait, like a seductive woman."

"I see what you mean," said Kate, fascinated. "And the target comes to it—"

"—*penetrates* it," said Jessie.

Kate giggled. "Watch out for mines and loose women with V.D. Hey—V.D.: vagina dentata! The trap with teeth."

Jessie was not smiling. "But these things have no self-starting power. That's what makes them seem female. They never go off by themselves."

"Have to be touched off," said Kate thoughtfully. "The man with the box has to make the bomb explode."

Jessie nodded. "So you see, none of them are really female weapons. They're men's nightmares about what women could do to them, even if they carry guns."

"Mm," said Kate. "But what would be a real female weapon?"

"I don't know," said Jessie. "That's what I've been trying to figure out. A sponge, maybe. Or some kind of suctorial device."

"I can see it as a movie—this giant vacuum cleaner sucking up Tokyo."

"I'm serious, Kate. All the natural destroyers use female energy—quakes, volcanoes, whirlpools, cyclones. Even ocean currents. Powerful sucking devices in a female form."

"Mm," said Kate, trying. "They all move in circles, or ooze or explode. They're all sort of rhythmic. . . ."

"And think of the noises," Jessie went on. "Crying, howling, shrieking. Woman sounds, right?"

"Hysterical," said Kate. "Banshees and Furies. I think you've got something, Jess. Have you written the patent office?"

"Well," sighed Jessie, "you have to admit it's interesting. Nobody understands how any of those things work. Men can't control them, can't figure how to adapt all that energy for practical use. They shoot bombs into volcanoes, and it makes

47

them worse. I've even read that Yugoslavian farmers shoot rockets into thunder clouds. They haven't the foggiest idea which cloud is dangerous."

"I kind of like the sponge idea," Kate mused. "Soft when wet, without losing toughness. And they can absorb anything, within reason. If we get to choose our weapons, I'll take that."

"You could do worse," said Jessie. "Did you know the sponge can reproduce sexually or asexually? All the cells—eggs and sperms—just swim around in a mass of larvae?"

"No, really?" said Kate. "I love it."

Chapter 4

FOR HER FOURTEENTH BIRTHDAY, Diane Waterman had her
heart set on a pair of silver shoes with four-inch platform soles.
She had no possible use for them, living on a rock at the end
of an island, but she took a fierce pride in her feet and ankles
—her slimmest parts—and nothing would do but these particular shoes. They were not really silver, of course, not the
dull, well-bred silver of classic kid dancing pumps. More of a
clear plastic laminate impregnated with a thousand shiny
metallic flakes—shredded Christmas tinsel preserved in aspic.
The shoes would shine at her feet like emergency flashlights
signaling a wreck. They had been advertised in newspapers
and magazines after a flamboyant male singer of the period
appeared in them at a concert. His were a twinkly red, however—magic ruby slippers like those the good witch Glinda of
Oz had commended to Dorothy, in a vain attempt to keep
her out of trouble. Diane had considered carefully, and decided
that the silver would be more refined.

Actually, she never expected to wear them outside of the

house. Certainly not to Andrea Island Junior High School, where she was already considered peculiar. Her lethargy in class, her perpetual air of sullenness, her excellent grades, and her distinctly city accent had all set her firmly apart from her classmates—towheaded farm children, blacks from the villages' poorer areas, and the youngsters of prosperous small shopkeepers whose success had always depended on summer people like the Watermans, and who therefore despised them. Even if she had not been strange, Diane would not have made it out there.

Neither she nor Robin had ever been invited to visit a classmate's house after school. Robin had made several attempts to invite girls home with her, but their mothers had declined in a way that established a general policy. The Watermans lived too far, it was explained. At the beginning, Robin had cried, but Diane pretended not to care. And after a while the family stopped expecting the situation to change. Jessie came to look at it as a sign that they were meant to remain outsiders—as if, having once chosen exile, they ought not to temper it by trying to glide into the mainstream of any other community's life.

Kate had been with them several days before Diane decided she was still safe to talk to, even with Jessie around, and from then on she would not leave Kate alone. She wanted Kate to come to her room, help her with homework, listen to her secrets—the more presentable ones. She told Kate about her passion for Latin poetry. She wanted to *be* a Latin poet. "*Odi et amo,*" she recited. "I hate and yet I love." She also loved mythology, and legends about brave, doomed women whose heroism and whose undoing were invariably linked to some physical or sexual deformity, often self-inflicted. Was it true, Diane wondered, that Joan of Arc never menstruated? And how did anyone *know*—had she told people? Her soldiers? Her inquisitors? Wasn't it possible that she *had* menstruated, and then stopped because she'd been wounded or frightened—like girls in Nazi prison camps; like rape victims?

And what about the goddess Diana, her namesake, cutting off her breast so that her quiver of arrows would lie flatter against her body—not to impede her swiftness when she hunted. How did the wound heal? Was there a scar? Of course not, Diane answered her own question. Diana was a goddess. Had there really been a woman Pope who got pregnant? Kate didn't know; Diane didn't expect her to know. She only wanted Kate to know that she was interesting.

Diane talked very little about her father, who had always frightened her, but she talked even less about Jessie, whom she idolized. Jessie found it remarkable that the girl seemed to "open up" so easily with Kate. She was usually tongue-tied with strangers. With everyone, in fact, except Jessie. Kate was already aware of that; she had noticed Diane's eyes following Jessie's every movement, like the eyes of a novelty religious portrait. Sometimes Kate would come upon Diane standing in the hallway outside the door of Jessie's bedroom. Just standing there, not even close enough to eavesdrop. "I was—" she would say, and then dart away mumbling, and lock herself in her room.

Or they would all be together in the living room, reading, and Kate would look up and catch Diane studying Jessie, copying the way Jessie sat with one foot tucked under her, or the way she frowned in concentration, or twisted her ring when she was bored, or absently touched her hair. It was a cannibalistic process, Diane's memorizing of her stepmother. She did it with the photographs as well as the living model. Absorbing sections of Jessie—her different smiles, her gracefulness, the way she shaped her fingernails. As if the girl were assembling the sections in some way for her own use. She must practice in her room, Kate thought. Harmless, probably. Kate remembered doing that herself when she was a teenager. With movie stars. By the time the movie ended, Kate

51

had become the heroine. She had not only learned every gesture; she had, in effect, swallowed the character whole so that her perfection gleamed through Kate's eyes and the pores of her skin. Leaving the theater, Kate always knew she had changed—*knew* it. Her features, her body, her voice. And if someone spoke to her, called her by her own name, she would start as if she had been struck. Don't call me that! she would rage at them silently. Couldn't they see she was not that person any more? She would have to shut her eyes to lock her transformed self inside for safekeeping, until she could be alone. She had to thread her way carefully through the brightly lit theater lobby, along the street. There might be mirrors or plate-glass windows. A shiny car might shatter the illusion. She would force herself to hang back from the crowd of ordinary people in drab and rumpled clothes. She would hide from everyone who could not see her clearly, who could not recognize the change that had occurred. Fools, she would cry to them, I am among you, but no longer of you. I shine. Don't touch.

That must be what Diane was up to, Kate thought. That must be it.

She was at least partially right. Diane played many parts. When Roy was around, for example, she played Daddy's girl. She could no longer play it so convincingly as Robin, but it was still the role she knew best. As Roy's first girl child, she had learned it almost from birth. Roy's seductiveness operated as smoothly with his daughters as with other females. Perhaps more smoothly. He would be talking to Diane gravely about school, or even shouting at her about some gross misdeed, when suddenly he would remember that she was his *daughter*. The change in his voice, in his expression, would seize him like a facial tic, and he would demand that she come and hug him, or kiss him, or sit on his lap. Then he would begin to tease her—about getting fat, getting a *figure*. "Look," he would say, and cup his hands around her hips. He would gaze at her bosom, or pinch her arms. He would shake his head in wonderment.

They were both embarrassed by this uncontrollable need he had to discuss her in physical terms. It was as if they had an understanding—he needed to joke about her body in order to place it at a safe distance from his own. It was a disclaimer of carnal interest, and at the same time a statement of ownership. Part of the problem was that Diane looked like her father—the same solid legs; the large, intelligent face; strong features, smoke-colored eyes, curly hair. Not beautiful, but living proof of the power of his sperm, the dominance of his genes. I know she's not beautiful, he seemed to protest, touching her, deprecating her. She's not what I would choose for myself—even if she weren't my daughter.

Jessie's child Robin bore no resemblance to Roy at all; she was a microfilm edition of her mother, and Roy was enchanted by that. If he touched Diane, he could not stop touching Robin. He could not speak to her without picking her up, ordering her to put her arms around his neck, to squeeze, to give him a hundred kisses, to ride on his back. But she was nearly nine years old, not a baby, and she often ran from him, crying, No, Daddy, I don't want to—you can't make me.

As with his treatment of adult women, his handling of daughters had once been the norm for daddies; now it was frowned on. Foolish, certainly, if not offensive. Probably unhealthy. Yet he was helpless to change it. Or rather, he refused to see that he ought to.

Robin's sole source of pleasure lay in her vast collection of foreign dolls, each of which wore some traditional native costume. She did not play ordinary games with these elaborate creatures. She never rocked them or fed them or changed their clothes or set them about in houses. Mostly she catalogued them, like a prim librarian, according to size or in alphabetical order of their countries. She labored over index cards, setting down dull information about each doll and its background. Date and manner of acquisition; description of costume, of hair; skin color. The cards were filed in boxes. She was never satisfied with the filing system, but constantly revised and improved it, destroying old cards and making out new ones.

Sometimes she rearranged the dolls themselves, carefully removing them from their shelves, inspecting and regrouping them according to some new plan, and then putting them back. Often she added notations on their cards to indicate some news event in the country they represented. Wars, famines, revolutions, declarations of independence, assassinations of leaders.

Frequently Diane would help her sister, though Robin disliked anyone else touching her dolls. Diane had been the one who thought of index cards, and also volunteered her typewriter. Robin had previously written everything in colored pencil, printing each word with painstaking care. She adopted Diane's innovations and followed her instructions, but grudgingly, the way a puppet ruler of an occupied territory follows the advice of a powerful benefactor. The power is an illusion based on outside interference, but the "ruler" sustains pride by choosing what kind of help to accept, and on what terms.

So Diane would come in with her typewriter, and Robin would let her suggest what to put on the cards. Population of native country; drawing of flag; description of currency; mode of government; name of current head of state. After Diane left, Robin would scrutinize her work, discarding with quick, fierce gestures any contribution Diane had made without consulting her. Once Robin discovered a set of color photographs in the file; Diane had surprised her sister by taking a series of portraits of each doll. Full-length, profile and close-up of the face. Naked and in costume. It was a wonderful idea. Robin tore up the photographs without saying anything to Diane. But she continued to let her older sister come and help with the cataloguing.

It was nearly a week before Roy's first letter arrived. Post-marked Paris, although the stationery bore the name of his London hotel, which he'd left three days before. Roy was not much for cabling safe arrivals. It was, in fact, unusual for him to write at all except when he was about to come home and wanted to be met at the airport or have a decent dinner waiting.

"Dearest J," he wrote. "Your face pursues me—old magazine covers in hotel rooms. Your eyes reproach me from torn billboard posters. Part of myself torn away too. I feel—ah, Jessie, goddamn it, I do love you so. If all goes well, deals should be closed in two weeks, three the most. I count the milliseconds.

"Can't stop hating the fact that Kate S. is there with you— she *is* there still, isn't she?—and I'm not. How I wish you were alone, missing me on our island. Waiting for me. I can almost feel you now, circling me, sealing me in. Tighter. There. Kisses for R. and D. And for you, different kisses. Hide them in secret places on your person. I'll find them somehow. You know how. Soon. R."

There was a violent electrical storm that night; Jessie said such storms occurred all the time out there. They all sat in the dark living room, watching the lightning tear the sky and the rain unfurl like sodden banners. Gusts of wind rattled the glass walls as though demanding concessions. They could have been on an ark, the four of them. The two girls sat quietly, their faces unreadable. They did not seem frightened, merely resigned, like children in a dentist's waiting room. Jessie, however, was in a state of high excitement. She paced and drank cold coffee; she talked incessantly about the storm, about flood damage, about how vulnerable the house was to high wind and swollen tides. Sometimes when the power lines were hit it took days to restore electricity. Often the roads were flooded for a week or more. None of the other houses in the area were occupied during the winter, and the telephone lines were always the first to go. There would be no school if the bus couldn't run. The freezer was stocked, but if the electricity were off for any length of time. . . .

There were two spots of high color on her cheeks; whenever a flash of lightning illuminated the room, Kate saw them glowing like live coals.

Hours later, the lightning had stopped, though the storm did not abate, and Jessie thought the girls should go to bed. "Enough excitement for one day," she said, though it clearly was not enough for her.

She and Kate stayed up most of the night, as they once had so many nights in school, drinking wine and saying unforgivable things about absent friends. Congratulating each other for being true and sublimely clever and probably the last real people on earth, so wasn't it lucky they were out there together, orphans in the storm. They laughed a great deal; neither of them could have explained what was funny; everything was, insanely funny. They ate their way through a mountain of imported cheese and a sea of homemade vanilla ice cream; they filled their mouths as if in terror of leaving them empty, after all the foolish words and meaningless laughter had been poured out. They were drunk, they supposed; on sleeplessness and the storm and darkness and isolation. And Kate supposed she was a little drunk on Jessie.

At one point, without thinking, Kate asked if Jessie still hated her breasts. Jessie was astonished that she remembered. They had always talked about breasts in school—everyone they knew hated something about her own breasts: the size, or the shape, the heaviness or the proportion, the pointiness or lack of pointiness. Jessie's breasts belonged on a Botticelli Venus, but Jessie hated them. Nothing *about* them, just the fact of having them at all. She told Kate—and Kate reminded her now—that she never let anyone touch them, not even boys she went to bed with. Kate had never asked Roy about that, though she had often thought of it. Breasts were very important to Roy. Also to Kate. Every one of Kate's best fantasies had to do with her breasts. Having them exposed and stared at; having them discussed by admiring strangers; having them insured for a million dollars. In her wilder dreams, Kate's breasts had inspired reverent gasps from artists, rapists, cops, rogue priests, jaded gynecologists and nationwide television audiences.

But Jessie's breasts—*Jessie's* breasts had now, all at once, begun to inspire Kate. The outline of them, under her thin white shirt. The movement of them when she breathed.

Robin cried out in her sleep that night. "We'll all die," she cried, "if Daddy doesn't come back. He's not coming back. I know he's not!" She began to rock vigorously in her bed and suck her index finger—habits she was thought to have outgrown. At first Jessie tried to soothe her, but the child sucked harder, and rocked harder. Jessie grew angry then, partly because Kate was there, witnessing this. The toothmarks on Robin's finger were deep lacerations, almost as deep as if she had been bitten by an animal.

Only a desperately unhappy child would bite herself so hard, Jessie was sure. Only a bad mother would have a child unhappy enough to bite so hard. "Don't cry," Jessie said, rocking her child.

"But we'll all die," sobbed Robin.

"No," said Jessie firmly, "we won't."

When Robin was a baby, they had employed a nurse who routinely administered tranquilizers by rectal suppository. Jessie had discovered the package one day in the medicine cabinet. "Pediatric dose," it said on the label. "What are these?" she asked the nursemaid. It turned out the woman had a standing order with a pharmacist in the neighborhood, a young man with violent pimples, whom she spent the night with sometimes on her day off. Robin was a very tranquil baby. She had never been so tranquil since. Jessie sighed. "Stop it, now, Robin," she said, without conviction. She closed the door quietly and went back to the living room with Kate. The rain continued.

On the second night of heavy rain, the girls went to their rooms earlier, and without prompting. As if, like one of their own tantrums, the bad spell would be over soon if they ignored it. "Don't encourage her," Roy used to say when any of his children "carried on." Jessie had always tried not to encourage them.

That night Jessie and Kate sat in silence; the torrent outside at last seemed eloquence enough. Even the lightning now flashed only occasionally, in silence—there was no more thunder. The skies would simply open, like doors swinging wide on invisible hinges, and the women would look at each other in the sudden brightness, and smile.

A strand of hair hung over Jessie's eyes. Kate reached out to smooth it back and Jessie's hand lifted, as if someone else had raised it, and took hold of Kate's, and held it against her cheek. Kate moaned softly and Jessie said, "Ssh, it's all right, I want you to," and so Kate kissed her as if they had always been lovers; as if it were the most natural thing in the world.

Then Kate murmured, "I don't know why I'm doing this," and Jessie laughed. "If we do it a little more, maybe it will become clearer." And so they went on, amid the flashes of silent lightning, and enveloping darkness, mouths touching each other slowly, reverently, like the blind learning flowers.

"Lean back," Jessie whispered, sliding her hand under Kate's long dark hair, lifting it and spreading it across the sofa pillow. Her fingers drifted through the hair like the teeth of a heavy velvet comb. Kate felt the drifting along her arms, her legs, the base of her spine. It was a current; an undertow. "Jessie," she said, "you don't know what I feel." The fingers paused where they lay, entangled in Kate's hair. Jessie's light-filled face came toward hers, upraised on the sofa pillow. Jessie whispered into Kate's mouth, "Of course I do." Jessie's lips were parted; Jessie's tongue glistened like a red-gold flame.

They undressed quickly in the darkness and found each other without ever losing the way. Then they lay quietly waiting for the flashes of light to confirm what they had already learned—that it was good to be loved like this, on a warm, wet night, by a friend. They fed each other tastes of themselves, mingled essences of chypre and musk and oakmoss, until it was all blended into a single rare perfume. So this is how Jessie tastes, Kate thought. Not butterscotch, after all. "What are you thinking?" Jessie asked. And Kate smiled. "About tasting you." "Mmm," said Jessie. "Good?" "So good," said Kate.

But Jessie would not touch Kate's breasts, and she would not let Kate touch hers. "Why not?" Kate asked, in a teasing whisper, to make light of it. "I mean, what is the point of a woman lover if there are no breasts?"

"Because I hate them," Jessie said softly, and bent her head so that her mouth brushed across Kate's thigh, and hovered close to Kate's center, waiting. "I love you here," she said. "Isn't that enough?"

Still, for Kate it was painful to make love that way, with forbidden zones. If she so much as grazed the outer limits of a breast with her lips or fingers, Jessie's body grew taut under her, and pulled away. Yet the rest of Jessie was pliant and yielding; she melted under Kate's touch, and Kate felt absurdly grateful that Jessie allowed her to touch her body at all. That first time, that wondrous first time, Kate felt her first genuine rush of overpowering rage at Roy. Because he owned this body and felt no special awe, no humility. Had he ever felt awe? Unthinkable. To Roy this was merely body of wife; comfort station; home.

Jessie was not thinking about Roy. Jessie was thinking about B. G.—her black gunman. Jessie never ceased to think about B. G. He had touched her here—and also here. B. G., caressing her breasts with his gun. Her breasts; inviolate white-gold treasures that she permitted no one to touch in love. How fitting it was, his gun as *her* symbol, as trigger mechanism for the implosion of hate inside her. But it was Roy she hated, wasn't it? She kept trying to remember. If Roy had stroked her breasts against her will. If she endured that special ravishment at Roy's hands, Roy's tender hands. If she granted it as a conjugal right, however it wronged her. Roy's lips, Roy's cock? Caressing, gliding over her like this? Or the cold steel of B. G.'s rod. B. G. . . . B. G.? *I hate Roy.*

And there had been a sharp rasping sound. Yes—hear it? There; unmistakable. A definite click. Of a key in a lock? Of a gun inside her mouth—inside her body? The click of a trigger cocked; a cock, triggered . . . Roy? Jessie? Ahh—and then the ragged tearing; the sharp black/red, ah . . . ah. Roy's homecoming. Roy's coming . . . home. (Scream again, Jessie. Ah. Ahh.) And then the sound of something running down the darkness; a final sigh.

Kate closed her eyes, and Jessie touched the fluttering lids gently, with her Kate-scented fingertip. Then she kissed them. She felt a rush of tender sadness, sensing that there would never again be such simple erotic pleasure between them. There was too much at stake. The test of whether she had reached a point of no return, of whether she could pass it without looking back. Would she be free, then? Would she know? There was still so much to learn. She needed to love Kate a different way, a very different way.

Thinking about it, Jessie felt the inner churning again. Excruciating pressure. Painful enough to make her cry out, but she could not. Kate must never suspect . . . whatever it was. Jessie thought, How does *she* stay alive in there? I give her nothing to feed on. So still for so long, I almost thought she was . . . gone. But she does that to torment me. Bitch.

The following day, there was no rain. The sky was leaden and the air steamy. Very odd weather for November; the island seemed huddled in a warm, soggy blanket, waiting. The series of heavy rainstorms had flooded all the main roads and washed out most power lines. Schools were closed, and many residents remained in their homes, overcome by torpor. There seemed no point in moving, and in any case, the heavy gray air was discouraging, a portent.

The Waterman house, situated on a flooded road at the far end of the island, was marooned. Kate and the two little girls had no sense of danger. Jessie seemed unusually restless, and would disappear for long periods, attending to mysterious chores. She did not ask for any help.

At dinner, Diane asked Kate if she would come to her room some time and look over the Latin poems she had translated that afternoon. Kate had complimented her on previous attempts with Catullus; his anguish seemed to blend well with the pain of a modern adolescent. Kate said she'd love to see the new work some time. Later that evening Kate passed Diane's room, found the door open, and peered in. Diane was seated in her desk chair, naked except for her new silver shoes. Her back was to the door, and she had moved the chair away from her desk so that she was facing a long mirror attached to a closet. Kate watched her, watching herself, as she masturbated. Each of her legs hung over an arm of the chair, and she was motionless except for one hand that moved in a stately rhythm at her center, like the automatic pen of a child's Spirograph soundlessly tracing precise red and blue circles at the touch of a button. Her eyes closed briefly and then flew open; at the moment of her release, her knees pulled upward like the hinged limbs of a jointed cardboard acrobat, responding to a tug of the single string that controls its limited repertoire of tricks. She hung there briefly, as if she had been wounded or were posing for a camera. Kate realized she was studying her own climax; noting the position of her breasts, the look of her mouth slightly open, and the pose of her feet, which now pointed upward and away from her seated body like dead shiny birds in awkward suspension, symbols of arrested flight. Her feet, with those grotesque silver weights strapped to them, immobilized in midair, in-

capable of supporting the body that now shuddered and subsided gently in place. Suddenly Diane's eyes caught Kate's in
the mirror. Neither of them spoke. Kate wondered why the
child did not seem startled; later it struck her that she must
have known how long Kate had been standing there; must
have known her door was open; must have, in fact, left it open.

Chapter 5

ROBIN WAS PLAYING with her dolls. Or, rather, playing with one particular doll—Catherine the Great. Lately, when she was alone, Robin had begun to do more than catalogue and file. She had begun to act out historical scenes involving dolls that represented real individuals, not just types. On that second night of the storm, Robin was plotting Catherine's accession to her husband's throne. She had put Catherine to bed, in her royal summer palace. There the doll was tossing and murmuring in her royal sleep. "For eighteen years," Robin murmured, "I have led a life . . . all I do is read, ride horseback, dance and have lovers. Others in my place would have gone insane by now. Or died . . . of melancholy."

Robin left Catherine to her troubled dreams, and placed Captain Orlov at the foot of the bed. "Yes, Captain Orlov? What is it? You woke me up!"

"Little mother," said Robin, affecting a deeper, Orlovian tone, "the time has come."

Robin yanked off Catherine's covers, pulled her out of bed, and dressed her up in a soldier's uniform.

"Not bad," said Captain Orlov. "Now go lead your troops to confront your husband, and tell him you're taking over the empire. Hurry up."

"Don't tell me what to do," said Catherine in an imperious tone. "Or I'll lock you up in a cage, like my friend Natalya did to her hairdresser."

"And why did she do that, your Majesty?"

"Because," said Catherine, "he knew too much. He knew she wore a wig."

Robin placed Catherine on her black horse in front of her troops. She put Emperor Peter on his royal yacht. "Catherine will never catch me!" he cried. "I'll sail to my fortified island." Robin whisked the getaway yacht across her turquoise shag carpet to Peter's secret island fortress. She placed an armed guard on the shore to greet him. "Who goes there?" the guard shouted. "The emperor!" Peter replied. "Oh, yeah?" said the guard. "There is no emperor. There is only the Empress Catherine. And you're under arrest."

Robin threw Peter into his island palace, surrounded by guards, and hurried back to change Catherine's costume from a military uniform to a black gown. Then she seated the empress at a writing table and placed a letter in her hand. ". . . poor Peter was fighting at the dinner table again, and all of a sudden somebody killed him. Nobody knows who gave the order, little mother. Sorry about that. Signed, Orlov."

Robin sighed and moved Catherine to her palace balcony. She assembled a crowd of Russian peasants. "My husband is dead!" Catherine shouted to them, waving a handkerchief. "Isn't that terrible?" "Dead of what, your Majesty?" shouted the peasants. "Oh, colic, I think," said Catherine. "Now hail me, or else!"

"Long live the empress!" shouted the peasants.

"Whew!" said Catherine. "Wasn't I great?"

Within minutes after Hurricane Minerva sprang to life full-grown and in battle armor, 500 miles out at sea, she had been photographed. A beautiful monstrous creature, still changing her shape, arranging herself artfully, her curving white arms reaching out, her inner ring of silver clouds tightening. Strangely beautiful monster, with an unmistakable identity. She was remarkably photogenic, like a pale spiral galaxy whirling breathlessly through space.

She was the one the hunters were going to get. They would fly straight into her center, into the engine of the storm, equipped with the most sensitive equipment ever designed by man to penetrate a hurricane. They had instruments to measure her moisture, her warmth, her coldness. They had computers trained to imitate her movements, thermometers they could drop like bombs into her seabed, and silver smoke they could blow into her eye to regulate her angry weeping. Most important, they would probe the source of her energy, the vortex at her core where she was most violent, screaming and whirling, and capable of incredible destructive strength. Once they understood the force that drove her so mad, it was assumed that she could be controlled. She could be made to do what they wanted her to do. They would capture her and make her civilized. There must be some way they could use that prodigious energy of hers. Let her water their crops. She could be trained to pull up the sea, spin it around inside her, wash the salt out and give it back to them as nice clean rain. They would find something to keep her busy. Something . . . harmless.

Strange that I should still be sleeping so soundly, Jessie thought. It won't be long now. Somehow she knew Minerva was coming. She felt it as though it were part of her, as though its power were in touch with her own, with the violent engine turning inside her. Somewhere in her own inner space, protected and hidden behind thick, dark-red walls. Shining. She felt something new moving there now—alive and moving, armed and dangerous. Should put up a sign, she thought, smiling to herself in the dark. Enter At Your Own Risk. Or possibly, Do Not Enter. It would, of course, make no earthly difference.

In the eye of the storm, she knew, it would be utterly still. They would be dead center, encircled by angry water and fierce swirling wind. Furies released. But deep inside, it would be silent as a womb; she would have to see to that. Maybe we should rename it, she thought. Cunt of the storm. In any case, she was confident they would survive. She would know what had to be done. She would have to make allowances for the interference; she sensed that there would be interference— stormbusters with the latest "techniques" for modifying a storm's behavior. Treating her like a madwoman, Jessie thought. Tearing a hole in her, miles wide. Dosing her with chemicals to calm her down. They would bottle their ejaculate in bomb casings and send it flying into her warm center. The bombs would go off in there, setting fire to her. It had been done successfully a number of times. Gang rape as a tool of basic research. Twelve of them, thirteen—all heroes—attacking her repeatedly at regular intervals. Some would deposit the seed, the rest would hover there. Monitors. Voyeurs. They would tame the bitch; that was how they thought of it. They knew if they could hurt her enough—if they could change her internal form—she would weaken. She would destroy herself.

Chances were they had already begun to stalk her. Tracking. Learning her rhythm, her movements. Know the enemy, they told themselves. But she wouldn't know about them. When they were coming, or from where, or how many times. Fair game.

Jessie understood the hurricane hunters. They had to pierce that secret center—where it was bright and warm, serene and beautiful. They had to get in there, and the only way was to pierce the tough protective walls. Break her down. Force their way through that dark, wet ring that guarded her center with such ferocity. They loved her when she was angry.

The storm would defend herself. Fight them off by pulling at their rivets, beating at their windows. She would try to tear them apart. Jessie knew how hopeless that would be. They would only shake their heads and smile, and make another pass. Some dangerous sport, they would say, pleased with her for playing hard to get. Jessie had read that the first man who ever flew into a hurricane had said, "Let's go and penetrate the center—just for the fun of it."

Kate lay awake in her white guest bed, sorting her feelings. An unsettling mixture of old guilts and new hungers. Not a sexual thing, she told herself firmly. How could it be? But then what was it? A freak accident; a single bizarre event that had nothing to do with either of their lives. Certainly not with hers. She had never imagined, never had the slightest . . . well, she admitted, that was not quite true. Women's bodies. She had always liked to look at women's bodies. Abstractly, of course. Paintings, photographs. The bodies of dancers, athletes, moving with exquisite grace on stages or film screens. She sometimes imagined herself touching such bodies. Thought of how they would feel, nude, moving beneath her hands. As a child, even then, she had liked to wander in sculpture galleries of big museums, gazing at the bronze and marble women. So cool, those immense perfect limbs. She remembered . . . reaching up and touching; fingers grazing lightly along a chiseled instep, in the fold of a low-draped garment. Beautiful, she had whispered to certain statues. If only you were alive, I would love you.

Nonsense, Kate thought now, nothing abnormal about that. Sculpture. The beauty of female bodies was a fact of life. Nude women were icons, national treasures. Everyone . . .

But the desire to touch, to caress—had it been erotic? Of course it had. Lust for the cool round limbs, the gleaming bronze bellies. She had longed to stroke the luminous buttocks

67

of Renoir bathers. She had wanted to lie naked with an Ingres odalisque. She had even felt an intense desire to fondle the opaline breasts jutting from the covers of men's magazines. Fondle—the very word excited her. Even women in cartoons —their full lips always parted, moist. Photographs of models in transparent lingerie, playing backgammon with invisible men. Offering themselves to the camera, the viewer. Women's bodies served forth like wonderful food. Yes.

But perhaps it had never been lust; perhaps she had only admired the perfection of those bodies? Abstractly, as she had admired Jessie's. Perhaps all she had wanted was to experience such a body. To have it—not the way a man "had" the body of a woman, by taking possession, invading it. But to have it—fuse it with her own. A synthesis of Jessie with Kate, Kate into Jessie. So that the whole would be both beautiful and hers to have. So that she could touch her own body and think, Beautiful. Mine.

Did that explain it, then? Kate's palms still tingled as if the electric touch of Jessie's skin had been imprinted on them. She closed her eyes and felt Jessie's warm breath on her eyelids, Jessie's hair sweeping gently across her face. With her fingers, she began to trace the course of Jessie's hands on her own body. There, she had touched, and like this. Yes, there.

She saw Jessie smiling, felt Jessie's hand guiding her own. This was how Jessie liked to be touched. She had learned all the colors of Jessie, and the soft sounds, and the textures. As if she had wandered into a closet filled with Jessie's clothes, in the dark, and taken handfuls of the warm silk, the soft fur, to press against her own skin, inhaling it, stroking it, wrapping it around her.

Not the breasts, though. Not the breasts. Why not? Kate heard her own voice again, pleading. Please, Jessie. Maybe tomorrow Jessie would allow it. Maybe just once. She would promise never to do it again. Just once. But maybe, if she were very gentle, Jessie would see, how softly—she would scarcely know what was happening. Butterflies, wings brushing, as softly as that. Kate whispered aloud, "Jessie, please, please let me—I need to, I'll do anything you ask, just let me."

How could Jessie refuse? How could she not want to be caressed like that? She must, Kate thought. Perhaps she was playing some kind of game. Perhaps she wanted Kate to be . . . more aggressive; take her by surprise—by force? Perhaps. Then that was what she would have to do.

Chapter 6

THE HOUSE ITSELF had sustained little serious damage from the driving rains that preceded Minerva, although at the foot of the driveway a fierce gust of wind attacked a pair of heavy wooden lantern posts. The posts now inclined slightly toward the ground, and the lanterns' glass panes were blown out, scattering splinters over the driveway like handfuls of rice at a wedding. The tops of nearby shrubs were sheared off, giving them odd new shapes, as if they had been clipped by a hostile bonsai gardener. On the road below the house, a small scrub pine leaned across a sagging telephone line, swaying and shuddering like an exhausted child caught in a makeshift swing. Finally, a loose piece of rock had broken off from the underside of the massive cliff on which the house perched, and toppled into the sea. Viewed in profile, the house now appeared to jut out at a more reckless angle over the high wild surf.

Kate Saville and the two Waterman girls still watched the weather impassively through sealed windows, a polite but restless captive audience at an interminable *son et lumière* festival. Jessie roamed the house, inspecting for damage; moving pots and wastebaskets under steady leaks; transferring perishable food to cooler, drier corners; collecting water in bathtubs and bottles; nailing shutters on the most vulnerable windows. She noticed some bubbles welling up from the concrete garage floor, but they soon subsided and she was not alarmed.

Kate thought they might have been experiencing nothing worse than a late spell of rough northeastern weather—a typical local disturbance that would soon blow over. And the elaborate precautions might have been an attempt to adapt, like the stoic natives of the area, who, they imagined, must be used to treating this sort of event as an ordinary nuisance— an impossible guest with regular visitation rights. Jessie did not bother to correct her; she did not want Kate frightened now.

Elsewhere, far to the south, deaths occurred. Houses were leveled and swept off beaches. People were evacuated from low-lying coastal areas as powerful winds gathered up the ocean, spun it around, and flung it across populated villages. Inland creeks and canals, swollen and overflowing, poured out over lowlands and marshes. States of emergency were declared.

Just to the north, in certain fishing villages, the sunset had such a strange rusty color that wary fishermen shook their heads and decided not to go out in their boats. Coast Guard tracking stations issued warnings and cautious predictions, based on conflicting signals from expensive weather satellites.

Jessie Waterman found an old tool belt in a utility closet, and took to wearing it slung low on her slim hips. It affected her posture and her walk. The elegant, long-legged, model's swing gave way to a stride. All her movements seemed touched with an altogether new kind of grace, closer to that of a natural athlete than of a woman accustomed to moving well under the demanding gaze of hot lights and strange men. She

71

might have been using a different set of muscles, or else the heavy tool belt caused a subtle shift in her center of gravity. What Kate noticed first was the accompanying change in Jessie's face. Suddenly there was no resemblance to the abstracted, troubled woman who had greeted Kate the day she arrived from the city. It was as if some singular personal cloud, at least, was lifting.

Jessie had noticed it, too, studying her mirror. Possible, she thought. One day I may even forget to look for *her*. In the meantime, though, she still saw . . . traces. Have to keep erasing, she thought, frowning at herself as though that would do it. As though she were covering up for some secret crime, some shameful mark of conscience. That would have been so much simpler. She would have to be patient. There was no way to eradicate the source of her pain, or the elaborate web of memories and reflexes that inflamed it. Without warning, it would act up like an old injury to the cartilage. Invisible even on the X rays, but undeniably there. Invisible scars would be the last to disappear.

Robin had removed all the male dolls from display. The African tribal chieftain, the Polish folk dancer, Scottish bagpiper in ceremonial tartan, Pygmy warrior, Eskimo fisherman, Swiss watchmaker, Sherpa mountain guide, Royal Canadian Mountie, Mexican peon.

First she had stripped off their costumes. Some, sewn onto the figures, had to be torn, since they were not designed to be removed for washing.

The information was duly recorded on the index cards. "Removed from display," Diane typed carefully, under Robin's direction. "Disposition pending."

"What are you going to do with the costumes?" Diane asked.

"Don't know yet," Robin replied. She planned a massive reorganization of the female dolls remaining on the shelves.

There would be no reference to national origins. She had assembled an elite corps of militant leaders Israeli commando, Cuban guerrilla fighter, Chinese Communist cell leader, American black radical . . . and a carefully selected companion group of historic figures—Catherine the Great, Joan of Arc, Cleopatra, Queen Elizabeth I, Judith, slayer of Holofernes, Catherine de Medici . . . She was considering whether the Lady Macbeth doll belonged in the group, on the ground that she had been responsible for murders. Diane pointed out that (1) she was fictional, and (2) she hadn't actually killed anyone herself, but only made her husband do it. Robin reluctantly agreed; no Lady Macbeth.

"It's too small a group, though," Robin said, frowning at them. "We may *have* to use the mythical characters."

Diane thought goddesses were okay, but not comic book creations like Wonder Woman.

"Wonder Woman is just as good as any old Greek goddess," said Robin defiantly.

"Stupid!" said Diane. "Why not Cat Woman, then? Why not Dragon Lady? And the witch from Hansel and Gretel!"

"Witches?" said Robin, thoughtfully. "Why *not* witches?" She began rummaging in her closet, where forgotten characters had been consigned.

Diane knelt beside the pile of discarded male dolls. They were heaped on the floor, face down, like victims of a massacre. She picked one up and turned it over. No penis. "Rotten way to be wounded," she murmured. None of them had a penis. They were all broad-shouldered, narrow-hipped, strong-biceped. Nowhere in the world was there a male doll with a penis. And nowhere but in the United States a female doll with breasts. Well, even there, not realistic breasts. Smooth, nippleless plastic spheres, hard as silicone; designed to "fill out" their clothes.

"What are you doing?" Robin shrieked. "You're *touching* them!"

73

"I'm sorry," said Diane, dropping the doll she held. He had been a Buckingham Palace guard, with a genuine fur busby. He clattered noisily, anonymously to the floor, among the other hard, smooth, penisless bodies. Diane and Robin watched him fall, impassively. Robin said, "Come on, let's get to work."

Jessie decided that all glass doors and windows should be nailed shut with wooden supports fastened across them. There was a limited supply of dry firewood in the garage, so the fire in the fireplace could not be kept going between meals. Once the meat was used up, they would have to eat most of their food raw. Still, there would be plenty of everything for several days—and by then the storm would surely be over.

Jessie asked Kate to help her remove a closet door and nail it up behind one glass window that had developed an ominous rattle.

"You know," said Kate, watching Jessie pound at the heavy door, "you look different. What do you think it is—me or the weather?"

Jessie laughed. But Kate drew her over to a mirror. "See?" she said. "Even your bones are sharper. Here—" She drew a finger along the fine, strong jawline. "And here too." She rested her hand on Jessie's cheek.

Jessie peered impatiently at her reflection, but without focusing. She already knew the differences. With her critical, all-seeing, model's eye, she had seen which lines now seemed subtly more distinct, as though a sculptor had clarified the shape of the skull. It was the kind of change that often comes gradually to the face of a soft blond woman if she ages well and has "good" bones. Planes and angles replace girlish round-nesses, and people begin to describe her as "handsome," meaning that she has ceased to be pretty. Not that Jessie had ever been anything so banal as "pretty." Still, the change was like that.

74

"You're imagining it," Jessie laughed. "Probably a result of your guilty conscience. Like kids thinking when a girl loses her virginity it changes the shape of her mouth."

"And the way she walks," said Kate, laughing too. "But I'm not imagining it."

"Well," said Jessie with an indifferent shrug, "then maybe my new exercises are finally working. If the rain lets up at all tonight, Diane and I will give you a demonstration. But first help me nail up one more door behind Robin's window. It's the last one."

"Why are you sealing this place up like a tomb?" Kate said. "I *like* watching the weather. It's exciting."

"That's because you haven't learned to respect it," Jessie snapped. Her tone was icy, a tone she often used now with Kate, and Kate winced as if Jessie had struck her.

"I wasn't really *complaining*," she said, not meaning to whine.

Jessie didn't answer her, but she laughed—an odd little laugh. Harsh. Kate didn't understand. It disturbed Kate, that laugh. Hurtful, and it made no sense. She felt chilled suddenly, aware that whatever Jessie felt for her was very different from—less than?—what she had thought. Their relationship seemed to have veered off sharply in a new direction, one whose course was being set, whether consciously or not, by Jessie. Kate, who seldom cried out of helplessness, felt the unpleasant sting of helpless tears. She would have to do something about this, she thought. She would have to master this game, if it was a game.

Jessie had begun to see it, finally. Not enough to dominate; there had to be the threat of violence. Implied threat, but constant. Blended with the sexual tenderness, so that there was no division, no way to tell where one ended and the other began. No way to tell that they were separable.

It could be done in such subtle ways. She knew that. Television newsman thrusting his microphone into the face of his subject. Subjecting her, so that she has to answer him, give him what he wants. She's a *willing* subject, but he controls her absolutely. She doesn't think he would hurt her, smiling, both of them smiling. But clearly he *could* hurt. Anyway, the subject was always willing. Everyone agreed to be the "guest." It was flattering to be chosen. You were desirable. Didn't matter about the control, "guests" never thought of that. Had to give whatever the host wanted. Jessie had seen inexperienced guests squirm, back away, talking too fast, being clever, trying to outwit. Cat and mouse game. They never screamed, though, You're hurting me. TV controls that too. Bleep it. TV smiles, thank you, puts away the microphone, that was a good "show."

Even the telephone, Jessie thought. Any impotent man can fuck strangers with a telephone. Easy. Hi, he says, friendly, into the receiver. Want to—? The ear is an opening. And the mouth. She said hello first, didn't she? Gave him an opening. And photographers. God, yes. Zoom lenses to shoot unarmed civilians. Close-up when they got used to it. They were always smiling. They *liked* it. Come on, they all like it. They actually beg for it! Take me, take me! Everyone asks for it. With a camera a man could do anything he wanted—get them to lie still, stretched out on paper. Get them to move and smile. He could take them in any position; they would hold it forever if he wanted. How was I? they would ask him anxiously, when he was through. Beautiful, baby. Really fine. Jessie smiled, thinking about that. She had been taken that way a million times.

Even women get to do it, she realized suddenly. To their children, when nobody else is looking. All they need is a spoon. Force the meat into the reluctant mouth, come on, down the gagging throat. Jessie had done it herself, sure she had, everyone she knew must have done it. Scraping the mess off the baby chin when it oozed out, pushing it back inside. Eat it, or else. Swallow it. Jessie had said that. She knew just how to say it. You have to swallow it because I say "or else." It didn't even matter what else. All that mattered was the voice, the tone, the control. And the baby knew. The baby learned to swallow it, so Mommy wouldn't hurt her. Good baby. Good Mommy. All she needed was a spoon; it was easy.

Jessie completed an oil pastel drawing that day, something she had been working on for weeks, feeling vaguely dissatisfied. It was a brilliantly colored design showing a pair of fantastic animals, more of a composite of fish, bird and human than any recognizable species, but distinctly a pair—male and female. The male, slightly larger, appeared puffed up and vaguely menacing. Its fins and tail were spread like arms and wings, and blurred to indicate rapid motion. In its talons was a pointed object; it was not aimed at anything, but merely resting across the male's body. The male's mouth was open, however, as though prepared to bark, or snap.

The female, less brilliantly marked and clearly not moving, bore a curiously intelligent expression—knowing. On a human face it might be read as fearful, submissive or cunning, but any of those would be an oversimplification. When she finished the drawing, Jessie added a written notation in the lower righthand margin. *Active exercise of control is necessary to establish and maintain social order.*

She stared at the finished work for a moment, and then picked up the black crayon to amend the notation. Between the words *of* and *control*, she added, in larger letters, the word *male*.

Chapter 7

ROBIN WAS PLAYING with Elizabeth I, whom she always referred to as the Virgin Queen. Diane had teased her about that, and she had replied seriously that only virgin women ever managed to wage war, lead troops into battle, or change history with their own hands.

"What about Catherine the Great?" Diane demanded.

"Well," said Robin, "first she had to arrange to be a widow."

Diane had never seen Robin fussing with her dolls' costumes before. She watched silently as the child stripped Elizabeth down to her royal petticoats, and then dressed her in a white velvet gown and a silver armored breastplate filched from one of her discarded male warriors. She had even removed the queen's red wig to fix white plumes and diamonds in it. After a few minutes, Diane nodded thoughtfully. "I myself will take up arms," she murmured. "I myself will be your general."

Robin grinned delightedly. "I have the body of a weak and

feeble woman," she said, "but I have the heart and stomach of a king."

The two girls quickly set up the queen's embattled army, her pages, her captain general and her master of the horse—all these parts played by female dolls—and finally set the queen upon her white horse. Robin had spent hours constructing a paper fleet of invincible Spanish galleons. She arranged them carefully now in a tight crescent formation. Diane set up the broken line of little English vessels. "Now," said Robin, "all we need is the great storm. Too bad we can't play outside. It's perfect—even the color."

Diane puffed out her cheeks, drew in her breath, and blew. The stately Spanish galleons scattered and toppled. Robin cheered and raised Elizabeth's right hand, with the silver scepter. "From now on," Robin said solemnly, "we rule the seas."

Diane smiled indulgently. "Actually," she said, "the storm didn't really defeat the Armada."

Robin flared. "Then why did both sides say it did?"

"Oh, because," said Diane wearily, "it made a terrific story. And the Spaniards figured it was better to have been sunk by a supernatural tempest than by a bunch of puny ships sent by an old woman. Even if she was a virgin queen."

Robin was about to cry, but she wouldn't. "Tomorrow," she said, "I'm doing Charlotte Corday the assassin. I already made Marat's bathtub and everything. And you can't play."

Diane shrugged. "Charlotte Corday was hopeless," she said. "Romantic and hysterical. I hate religious fanatics, they always kill the wrong people."

"She was not hysterical," Robin shouted. "Get out of my room." She brandished Elizabeth's tiny scepter as though it were a weapon.

"Shall I do it or shall I not?" murmured Diane, going. "*Le ferai-je, ne le ferai-je pas? Honestly*, Robin, you're such a baby."

Robin flung the scepter at the door and burst into tears. "I don't care," she sobbed. "Charlotte was a hero. They said, everyone said the blow . . . was skillfully dealt. *Skillfully dealt!* So there, shitty Diane." Robin took a deep breath, and repeated Charlotte's agonizing question as if it were a magic incantation. *"Le ferai-je, ne le ferai-je pas? Le ferai-je?* Yes, I will. I swear I will."

She stopped crying and went to retrieve the scepter. It was only slightly bent. Robin straightened it carefully and placed it back in Elizabeth's hand. Then she put the queen and her white gelding, the English fleet, and the Spanish galleons all back in their plastic shoeboxes, and went to the closet for Charlotte Corday. "I know what you'd say," she whispered fiercely to the doll. "One does not have to tell the truth to one's oppressors." She hugged Charlotte tight, then put her down quickly and began unwrapping the tiny dagger. "To-morrow," she whispered. "À *demain.*"

Alone in her room, Kate could still peek at the weather through the narrow slit of window Jessie had left exposed at the edge of the solid wooden backing. One thin stripe of day-light per room was enough to save candles, she said. Diane and Robin were enchanted with the idea of being sealed in; it was like a fortress. Indeed, each opening was barely the width of a loophole in a gun turret. For the first time, Kate felt imprisoned in this house, and frightened. Not so much of the storm as of Jessie, her friend, her lover, though she had no idea what it was about Jessie that should suddenly make her afraid. It was nonsense. Jessie was only behaving sensibly, as any intelligent woman would, with a family to protect. The danger was outside.

Must be your guilty conscience, Jessie had said to her. Guilt about what—Roy, had she meant? Kate was startled at the thought. Neither of them had mentioned Roy's name in days, nor had the children, not since the night when Robin cried for Daddy in her nightmare. Yet sometimes Kate felt he was still with them, still responsible for everything they did. She tried to imagine his eyes, watching her make love to Jessie, accusing her of seducing Jessie. "I did not," she protested aloud. *I want you to,* Jessie had said. And before, when Jessie had first invited her out here, she had said *I need you.* What kind of need? Kate had not stopped to question it then; why should she now? Had Roy suspected? Was that why he had been so set against her coming? She doubted it. Roy would never have thought . . . and besides, there was no reason to. Perhaps everything had simply happened without a fathomable reason—like the storms. Conditions have to be just right, and even then, not every cluster of clouds turns into a cyclone. There must be a coming together of causes—pressures building, unnatural isolation, a welling-up and, finally, an explosion. The explosion was really only the last step, the visible result. Anyway, Roy would probably be more amused than angry, Kate was sure. Amused, or maybe aroused. Possibly both at the same time. Lots of men enjoyed the spectacle of women making love to each other—they said so. Something about two nude women, setting themselves up for the man who's watching them. Kate pictured Roy laughing. Jessie would kill him. Kate smiled. Yes, Jessie might do that very thing.

Kate stood hesitantly at Jessie's door. Jessie? She was in the bathroom. I have to talk to you, Kate said. Come on in, Jessie called. She had a green towel on, covering her breasts. Hi, she said.

I wanted to ask you . . . Kate stammered. I wanted to know why, ever since. . . .

Ever since?

Ever since we, made love, you've . . . been acting as if you despised me.

Jessie was brushing her hair. Her eyes met Kate's in the mirror over her sink. How have I been acting? she said.

Kate looked away. As if I . . . you seem contemptuous. You snap at me. Cold. Or else you make me feel like—one of your children.

Jessie smiled. Come here, baby, she said. Kate.

Kate began to move toward her, obediently. Then she stopped. No, she said. There, you see, you're doing it now.

Come here, said Jessie again, caressing Kate with her voice. I want to hold you. I want. . . .

Kate smiled slyly. Let me touch your breasts, she said.

Jessie winced. I can't. You know I—

See? said Kate. If you loved me—

Oh, for God's sake, Kate. You're acting like a child. If I treat you like one, that's why.

Let me kiss them, pleaded Kate. Her voice was hoarse now, and she inched forward again, reaching.

Stop it, Kate. Jessie turned around to face her. The hairbrush clattered to the tile floor.

I'm going to, said Kate. You have to let me.

Stop it, I said.

You bitch! Kate screamed. You teasing bitch. She felt a terrible excitement.

Don't do this, Kate, please. I— But Kate lunged and in one quick motion tore the towel away and pinned Jessie's arm behind her back. Jessie fought her silently, fought the rising warmth of her own body. Kate knew her skin and would use it against her, was already using it. Jessie, yes, Jessie. . . . She grew slippery with heat, but still Kate tightened her grip, forcing her back and down against the cold tile. Kate's body pressed against her, crushing her, their faces blurring. Then Kate lowered her head slowly and took Jessie's breast in her mouth. God, she sobbed, oh, God, Jessie, I love you so.

For an instant Jessie lay stunned, letting Kate's mouth and hands claim her. Kate was moaning softly. Then Jessie lifted her free hand and raised it tenderly to Kate's hair, letting her fingers rest there. Kate, she sighed.

Kate's mouth was still on her breast, Kate's tongue, Kate's teeth, Kate's tears. Say you love me doing this to you, she murmured. Say you wanted me to take your breasts in my hands and put them in my mouth. Say it.

Jessie uttered a single cry, a short burst of tearing noise. Then she wrenched free. Kate, gasping, stumbled to her feet, one hand raised in front of her face in a gesture of terror. Jessie—

B. G., whispered Jessie. It was a curse or a benediction. A vow, an oath, a discovery, a confession. The sound exploded in Kate's ears with the force of a bullet.

. . . B. G. had caressed her breast with the gun. He had stroked her body with it, using it impassively, skillfully, as an instrument of pleasure. And she had responded. He had known she would respond; it was not surprising. They all did, he said. She had done what he ordered her to do with his gun; embraced it with her mouth, pressed it tight between her thighs. She had felt it entering her, smoothly. She had impaled herself upon it, like a virgin on a priapus. It would come. No, he had said. Do what I tell you and it won't come inside you. Do exactly what I tell you. Whisper to it. Like you loved it. Talk dirty to it. I promise it'll never come.

What should I call it? she had said. What's your husband's name? Roy, she said. Call him that. 'Cause that's what he is.

He had held it against her, letting her guide it herself, with her own hand. Sliding it, so easily, as if into a lubricated holster. Talk! he said. Tell Roy how good he feels in there. Ask him what he wants you to do.

Does it hurt? he asked her. No. Only let it be silent, hard and cold. A benevolent despot. She knelt and prayed to it, not to hurt her. She told it how handsome it was, majestic, black and shiny. Put her tongue inside its dark mouth to taste the burning, the sourness. Good? he asked her. Was it good? Ahh, she sighed. Ahh.

Jessie's exercises involved a long and elaborate ritual. The owner of the house, a physical fitness enthusiast, had filled a room adjacent to the garage—his secret torture chamber, Diane called it—with an assortment of sophisticated gym equipment ranging from mats, slantboards, chinning bars, stationary jogging machines and bicycles to a futuristic system of huge, grim-looking mechanical devices, each bristling with straps and chrome bars, padded leather cushions, weights and pulleys, all supported by giant metal constructions of cables and cogwheels, embedded in the floor. Each machine was designed to test and build the strength of a particular group of muscles—one for the upper arms and back, another for the chest and shoulders, a set of three for specific parts of the legs. A workout using the entire series could be completed in half an hour, but Jessie and Diane sometimes worked out together for over an hour at a time, and Diane often went back to the room alone two or three times a day. They had begun using the machines, mostly as a diversion, only a few weeks before Kate's arrival, but both of them had quickly grown addicted to the routine. Diane was especially proud of her emerging muscles and increasing strength. She had designed a program for herself with specific goals, and kept a daily log of her progress, recording body measurements, pounds of weight lifted, miles run or biked, number of hours worked, feats of strength or endurance mastered. It was a remarkable regime for a girl who only a few months earlier had been literally sleeping and overeating her way through adolescence. Still, as Jessie explained to Kate, the change was not entirely surprising. Diane had merely embarked on another binge, though the nature of this one was unusual for her. She had always been capable of ferocious dedication to her passing obsessions. Only the object of the passion changed—food, depression, sleep, poetry, sexual daydreaming. The *degree* of passion remained constant.

Still, this was the only time, so far as anyone knew, that Diane had ever fallen in love with anything that required hard and constant physical work. The results were undeniable. On the night Diane and Jessie first performed their exercises for Kate, Diane wore a dancer's costume of sleeveless black leotard and tights. Kate was astonished; the body she saw now bore little resemblance to the soft, heavy girl she had seen naked only a few days earlier. Diane was no slimmer, surely, but now she seemed rock-hard and amazingly powerful. Perhaps it was only the costume, and the sight of her chinning, with a set of heavy black iron dumbbells strapped around her hips, or lying on her back strapped to one of those giant machines, legs spread wide apart above her chest, then lowering slowly down to her armpits before thrusting a huge weighted bar up and away from her body, six or eight times, in a slow, aching, precise rhythm.

Jessie watched approvingly from the floor, where she was practicing intricate yoga postures. When Diane finished her work on the machines, she sat beside Jessie, placing her feet together as Jessie was doing, in front of her, sole to sole, so that her knees flared outward from her body. "I can't get them down," Diane said. "I've been trying for three days."

Jessie smiled. In the same position, Jessie was able to lower her knees effortlessly to the floor. "Try now," Jessie said.

"I *am*," said Diane. "They won't go down."

"Push harder," said Jessie. "Just to the point of pain. Then stay there—hold very still, right there—until you can force the pain to become . . . something else. Until you control it."

"I *can't*," Diane wailed. "It *never* becomes anything else— it just hurts."

"You're not giving it a chance," said Jessie softly. "You're not exercising the *will*."

"I *am!*" said Diane. "But it keeps hurting."

"*Control* the hurt," Jessie commanded. "Release it. You can change it into pleasure, peace, or power . . . whatever you want it to be."

"I can't, I *can't*," sobbed Diane.

Impulsively, Kate rushed over to the girl, knelt in front of her, and gently pressed her hands against the parted knees, trying to force them down.

"*Stop* it!" Diane shrieked. Kate pulled her hands away, horrified.

85

Jessie smiled, but did not move. "*You* can't force her," she said softly. "You don't know how to control another person's body."

"I thought—" stammered Kate. "I was only trying to help."

Jessie shook her head. "Force hardly ever helps, Kate," she said evenly. "Unless you know exactly how to apply it, and what will happen if you do."

That night Diane wasn't feeling well; cramps, she said. Not menstrual cramps, she added; just cramps. She wanted to lie down and have Jessie come and read to her.

Diane's room was dark. I don't want to use up candles for reading, Jessie said. I think we'll wait till tomorrow for that, all right?

All right, said Diane, if you'll stay and talk to me.

Jessie began to move the desk chair over to Diane's bed. No, said Diane. Sit here. She patted the bed. Otherwise I can't see you.

Jessie sat at the edge of the bed. I can't stay long, she said. Besides, if you have a stomachache you ought to sleep.

Could you rub my back? said Diane, turning over. Jessie slid her cool hands under the covers and began to rub gently. Harder, said Diane. Jessie pressed harder. Like this?

Mmm, said Diane.

Jessie rubbed another minute, silently, and then withdrew her hands, pulling up the covers and tucking them in tightly. Diane turned over. Are you and Kate lovers? she asked abruptly.

Jessie hesitated only a beat or two. What makes you ask that? she replied. Her tone was light. Diane could not read her face in the darkness.

Nothing, said Diane. I just wondered.

It's a very strange thing to wonder, isn't it?

I don't know, said Diane. But it's strange that you're not answering me.

The answer is no, said Jessie, with a quick laugh. Of course we're not. It was true. Of course, they were not.

Diane said, I wrote a poem about Kate yesterday. I've written lots about you too.

I know, said Jessie. Will you let me read them some time? Tomorrow?

Diane hesitated. I tore up the ones about you. Yesterday.

I'm sorry, said Jessie, carefully. I would like to have seen them.

I don't think so, said Diane.

Why not?

There was no answer.

Well, said Jessie, I think you ought to get to sleep now.

Kiss me goodnight, said Diane.

Jessie brushed her lips lightly across Diane's forehead.

Why did you do that? said Diane. I meant—

Go to sleep now, said Jessie firmly. Feel better tomorrow.

Jessie—?

Jessie paused at the door. Yes?

Nothing. Diane turned over again, so that her back faced the door.

Jessie stayed there. What is it, Diane, dear? Gently.

I love you anyway, murmured Diane huskily, muffling it in the pillow.

I love you too, said Jessie. Anyway.

Chapter 8

ON THE MORNING of November 18 the sun came out, pale
and uncertain, casting a peculiar milky light over Andrea
Island. The local weather bureau forecast was for more
drenching rain and strong, shifting winds, probably by mid-
afternoon. But of course, the Watermans did not hear the
forecast; their telephone and electricity had been cut off
for four days.

Minerva was still moving northward at a stately but relent-
less pace, radar and satellites dogging her heels like paparazzi
in pursuit of a reclusive movie star. Meteorologists had predicted exactly where (within 75 miles) and exactly when
(within twenty-four hours) she would strike the coastline.
Andrea Island was expected to be within her path, though
not until the following day. In any case, there was no evacua-
tion plan for the area, which was by then largely deserted.
There were no hurricane shelters, no embankments where
isolated families could flee to safety. The rocky cliff on
which the Watermans' rented cottage sat, so exposed and

seemingly so vulnerable, was in fact one of the highest, and therefore safest, spots on that end of the island.

Robin peered through her sliver of window and saw the sun. It was, she thought excitedly, a perfect day for the Great Terror. She could reenact a whole series of bloody scenes outside. There could be a guillotine, a tumbrel, a mob of howling fishwives; the walled convent where Charlotte Corday first dreamed of committing murder; the Marat assassination scene, Charlotte's arrest and execution. If she relented and let Diane help her, Robin could even stage the notorious Festival of Reason, with naked women whirling like mad savages as they desecrated Notre Dame. She could construct a Greek temple in the nave of the cathedral and have an opera-singer doll portraying the Goddess of Reason. . . . Robin bounded out of her room, flushed with excitement.

"For God's sake, Jessie," Kate was pleading irritably, "can't we take the blinders off the windows? The *sun* is out."

"No," said Jessie firmly. "Maybe in a day or two. Weather permitting."

"Can I take some of my dolls out and play near the Coast Guard station?" asked Robin.

Jessie frowned. "*Out?* It's flooded all along Ocean Drive. I don't—"

Diane cut in quickly. "We can walk along the rocks—and we'll wear bathing suits. *Please?*"

Robin glared at her sister. She had not even decided for sure whether to invite her.

"Well," said Jessie doubtfully.

"Oh, let them go," said Kate. "If it starts raining again they'll only be a few minutes' walk from the house."

"Well," said Jessie again, weakening. "I suppose if the two of them go—"

Diane grinned. "Come on, Robin," she said, with pointed condescension. "Before I change my mind about taking you."

89

"—but wear sweaters over the bathing suits," Jessie called after them. "It's still windy."

The two girls raced back to Robin's room and began packing dolls and equipment into canvas bags. "Don't forget the dagger," teased Diane. For once Robin refused to be baited. "We'll use the old gun pits at the fort," she said. Diane said no; the pits would be flooded. The ramparts, possibly.

Ocean Drive, before Minerva struck, had a beach club with a pool and bathhouses on the sea side, about two miles from the small town center of shops, post office, school, churches and library. On the bay side were the yacht club, marina and tennis courts. The road ran between them, stretching four miles out to Andrea Point and the Fort Monroe Coast Guard station, actually a detached lookout tower on the grounds of Fort Monroe, an old artillery post. The Monroe tower was an auxiliary station; the main Coast Guard unit for the island was nearly six miles away, on the opposite side of the town center. Fort Monroe itself, with its ramparts and concrete gun platforms, was a local tourist attraction; about half a mile from the Watermans' house, the only one of twenty-six houses along Ocean Drive that was still occupied fulltime at this time of year. Half the others were kept open year round and used for occasional weekends by their owners, but because of the unusually long spell of bad weather, these houses too had been closed and empty for two weeks.

Because of the flooding along Ocean Drive, Surfman Leo Bailey, the young coastguardsman stationed at Monroe tower that day, had had to leave his car at the main station and make his way to the tower in a patrol boat. He had been checking instruments and filing hourly reports to his captain over the Coast Guard communication system. At eleven o'clock, though the weak sun was still out, Bailey's captain had received a normal storm warning from the weather bureau.

Robin and Diane splashed along the water's edge to the old fort, climbed one of the parapets, and began to set their stage for Charlotte Corday's bloody mission to Paris. "First,"

said Robin, "we're doing Charlotte in her convent at Caen—
I brought nuns, and we can use—"

"What for?" said Diane. "Why can't we just start with
the assassination?"

"I wanted to do the mob killing a young officer right outside the convent walls. They cut his heart out with scissors—"

"Charlotte wasn't involved in that," said Diane disgustedly.
"The Marat killing was the only one she ever did."

"But it was a woman who ate that soldier's heart," Robin
protested. "Charlotte knew about it—"

"So what?" snapped Diane. "The scene is too much trouble
—all those clubs and pikes, and the mob was mostly men, and
anyway it wasn't important—it had nothing to do with
Corday."

"It was *so* important," shrieked Robin, on the verge of
tears. "It *inflamed* her. It had to do with her whole—motive
—her whole *idea* to kill Marat. I mean, before that she was a
schoolgirl in a convent!"

Diane laughed. "Honestly, Robin, you don't understand
revolution. *Everything* inflamed Corday. Everything was in-
flaming everybody. Violence all over the place, like . . . a
whirlwind. Old women hanging around the guillotine knitting
and cackling. You think Dickens made that up? Women
loved the blood. Some places there were nuns committing
atrocities. Mme. Lebon—"

"Oh, shut up," said Robin. "You think you know everything." Nevertheless, she reached into the bag for the Marat
bathtub.

"Where's Charlotte's scarf?" said Diane.

"What scarf?"

"She has to have a scarf for the arrest scene, and the execution too. They tore it off her—"

"I *know* that," said Robin, hunting furiously in the bag.
"I guess I didn't bring one."

"Honestly," said Diane. "I don't know why I even help
you."

Robin ignored her and began filling Marat's strange little metal tub with seawater. Diane watched her critically. "It should have a funny color, the water. And a funny smell. Mysterious steam coming out of it, from the disgusting stuff they put in it. You know, the medicine. He had scrofula or something."

"It doesn't matter," said Robin, setting the naked Marat into the tub, with the board set across his chest as a writing table, and a quill in his hand. "There," she said, pleased. "Now Charlotte comes in."

"I'd better—" said Diane, grabbing the dagger. "It has to be raised at a very precise angle. She drove it down directly into his heart. Like . . . this." Diane plunged the blade through the doll in the bathtub. "There!"

"The blow skillfully dealt," said Robin gravely. "They said it at her trial. That Charlotte did it like a professional assassin."

"Come on," said Diane, "they arrested her right away. They tied her to a chair—didn't you bring a chair either?"

"I must have—no, damn it, I can't find it."

"Well, forget it then. Did you at least remember the guillotine?"

"Here," said Robin, "and the tumbrel."

"What about Samson?"

"Who?"

"Samson. The executioner. He *drove* the tumbrel. He's the one who said to her, 'It seems like a long trip, doesn't it?' "

Robin smiled. "And Charlotte said, 'We'll get there eventually!' Wasn't she terrific?"

"Yes and no," said Diane. "She didn't even try to get away. She didn't even try to get Robespierre."

Robin ignored that. "It was raining the day they killed her," she went on. "A huge, sudden storm—"

Diane looked up as if she knew the sky would not miss its

cue. It did seem to be darkening. "Hey, look!" she exclaimed. "We'd better hurry up."

Robin was still fussing with Charlotte's dress. "Her dress was wet and clinging to her body—the crowd laughed at that."

"She had that same scarf on," Diane said. "They pulled it off—her shoulders were bare when she died. Come on, Robin, it's starting to pour."

Robin pushed Charlotte forward onto the wooden plank. "She *embraced* it," Diane cried. "Like a lover." She tied Charlotte's hands around the long board. "Now." She glanced at Robin. "Well, aren't you going to cut off her head?"

"Not really cut it off!" cried Robin.

"Why not? Squeamish?"

"No!" said Robin quickly. "I just don't see any point in ruining one of my best dolls. I might need her—"

Diane sighed. "You're hopeless, Robin. No guts."

"It's just not *necessary*." Robin reached out to untie Charlotte.

Diane seized her hand. "You didn't mind if Marat got stabbed. You didn't care about dismembering all those men the other day. And a few minutes ago you were ready to tear a soldier apart—rip his heart out."

"Yes," said Robin tearfully, "but this is Charlotte Corday."

Diane said nothing. Her smile, all pity and contempt, was unbearable. Robin drew in her breath sharply. "All right," she said. "I'll do it." She released the knife; Corday's head rolled into the basket; Diane cheered lustily on behalf of the bloodthirsty fishwives.

At that moment Coastguardsman Leo Bailey in the lookout tower checked his barometer and got a reading of 28.72, a sharp drop. He was trying to reach his captain to report it, when the system went dead. The wind had begun to whip the sea into froth, and heavy drops of rain were splashing into the already flooded concrete gun pits. A sudden gust picked up Robin's guillotine, the tumbrel, the canvas bag. Charlotte's headless body sailed off the parapet like a paper kite. "Come on!" yelled Diane, running. "The dolls!" Robin shrieked.

Up in the lookout tower, Leo Bailey saw black clouds racing across the sky and felt the huge panes of glass around him begin to shudder. Suddenly his feet were soaking wet; the ocean was seeping in. He stripped off all his clothing except for his trousers, hacking off the bottoms of those with his clasp knife. Then he raced down into the churning surf, hoping to get to his boat before the bow line gave way and it took off without him.

The two girls, up to their shins in water, were screaming at each other and running in different directions—Robin still chasing her scattered revolutionaries, Diane streaking down the shoreline toward home.

After the argument about the windows, Kate had gone to her room, saying she wanted to read and write some letters. "There's more light in the living room," Jessie had remarked. She was on her way down to the gym to exercise. Kate did not bother to respond, but walked quickly to her room and locked the door. Then, with a small hammer, she removed the boards Jessie had nailed to the sliding glass door that led to the sun deck, and settled herself outside with a deck chair, a blanket, pens, stationery and a magazine. She sat there for a while, feeling very daring, very exhilarated, for having defied Jessie. She dozed on and off. Then she began to write a letter, with no salutation. In it she confessed everything that had happened between her and Jessie—blaming Jessie, renouncing Jessie—and begged forgiveness from the unnamed lover for whom, presumably, the letter was intended. "Last night," she wrote, "I dreamed about you. Entering me like a thief in the darkness. It was cold and wet; I was floating stiff and silent in a pool of water, but as you approached, stirring the water, my body opened to you like a sea flower. And you took me. You—"

Kate never finished the sentence. As she was writing it, a sudden gust of powerful wind tore across the sun deck, toppling her off the deck chair. Within seconds, the deck was awash with rain and seawater, and Kate could barely make it back into the room. She tried to close the sliding glass door, but the force of the wind was too strong. "Jessie!" she screamed. "Jessie!"

Jessie, still downstairs in the exercise room, could not have heard her over the screaming of the wind. Besides, she had another emergency. Bubbles were welling up again through the concrete garage floor. This time she realized at once what they were—the ocean, seeping in. In a few seconds the floor of the garage was flooded under three feet of water. Jessie raced upstairs and began to nail the stair door shut, sealing the spaces around it with strips of metal she had been stockpiling —pieces of window screens and shower enclosures, window fans, pipes and ductwork she had ripped out of the wall of an unused bathroom. The job took her ten minutes. It was only then that she heard the screams and ran to Kate's room. Water was oozing out into the hall from under the locked door.

Surfman Leo Bailey thought he heard a child's voice, crying, before he spotted anyone. He was still trying to reach his patrol boat, bobbing crazily on the bay side of the watchtower. As he waded toward it through the swirling, rising water, he saw the rope break; the boat shot away from the dock as if its motor had been switched on. Bailey stood there in shock for perhaps a minute; then he heard the child's voice again, and turned back to investigate. By then Robin had tripped and fallen into the churning water of the gun pit; it resembled a whirlpool bath. Diane was nowhere in sight.

Bailey plunged into the pit and grabbed Robin's struggling body. He had dragged her to the edge of the pit and was pulling her out when the station collapsed behind them. The steel and glass tower, and its 100-foot radio mast, crumpled and sank into the bay. It made no sound at all.

The Coast Guard later pinpointed the time at about twelve thirty, some two hours before the peak of the storm.

Jessie had to smash the lock on Kate's bedroom door. Kate was still trying to close the sliding glass door to the sun deck, screaming and hurling her body against the force of the wind. Wordlessly, Jessie pulled her away. Bracing herself against the fixed pane of glass, she managed to force the sliding panel back across its track, inch by inch, making her moves only when the sound of the wind changed, indicating a slight shift in direction. Then she picked up the wooden boards and nailed them back into place. The white carpet was soaked, and water was still seeping into the hall. She seized Kate by the arm and pulled her out of the room. Kate was sobbing uncontrollably. Stay there, Jessie commanded. She went to get a metal strip for the bottom of Kate's door. When that had been nailed into place, she took Kate's hand and led her into the living room. Now, she said, why did you disobey me?

I thought—I'm sorry, Jessie, I thought it was safe—and you were just being—I don't know—mean. Stubborn about the windows. I was sick of being locked in, of the darkness. I didn't think there was any danger. I didn't—

Sit down, Kate, said Jessie quietly. Kate sank onto the sofa, still sobbing. Without warning, Jessie's arm rose and flashed; her open hand struck Kate's face. Kate stopped crying at once; she tasted blood, but she could not utter a sound. Do as I say, Jessie whispered tenderly. It was almost a croon, a lullaby. Do *exactly* as I say, and you won't get hurt.

Yes, Jessie, Kate replied, almost inaudibly. She was dimly aware that she was trembling, that her nipples were erect, that a pleasurable sensation of warmth and wetness was spreading between her thighs. Her head fell back against the sofa. Her eyes closed. The marks of Jessie's fingers glowed against her pale skin like scattered rose petals. Jessie stood there for an instant, watching her. Then she turned abruptly and left the room. It was not until she had gone that Kate remembered, with a start, about Robin and Diane having left the house. She began to whimper again, softly.

It took Leo Bailey close to an hour, half swimming, half wading, carrying Robin in his arms, to reach the house. Robin had been conscious when he picked her up out of the gun pit. "Where the hell did you come from?" he asked her. She told him her name and where she lived. Then she blacked out. He had no idea there had been another child with her.

When she saw them, Jessie stared blankly at her child, at the half-naked man: Just stood there staring, uncomprehending. Bailey misunderstood. "She's all right," he said, "just knocked out."

"But where's *Diane?*" Jessie shouted, trying to push past him.

"Diane? But I never saw anyone else."

"Her sister," Jessie said. "I've got to find her."

Leo Bailey shook his head. "Never make it now," he said. "Got to get you all out of here—"

"He's right, Jessie," said Kate. "Later we can go back, with a boat—"

"No! It'll be too late. I have to go now."

Kate held her arms out for Robin. Leo Bailey blocked the doorway. Jessie's eyes met his briefly. "All right," she said.

Leo Bailey had yellow eyes and a curly reddish beard. His wet trousers were plastered tightly to his glistening body. Kate quickly brought him one of Jessie's green towels. Jessie quickly brought him a pair of Roy's trousers.

Robin stared at him and for some reason thought of the arrogant young officer whose heart had been cut out and eaten by a woman, near Charlotte Corday's walled convent.

Leo Bailey said he thought the storm was Hurricane Minerva, and that even if it weren't, they must evacuate the house at once. He said he would be held responsible.

Jessie said he was welcome to go or stay, but that the rest of

97

them were staying. The house was prepared, she said. And he was in no way responsible.

Kate began crying again. "I can't help it, Jessie," she said. "I think we should go with Mr.— He seems to know—"

Jessie's eyes flashed. He knows nothing, she said. Nothing about this storm; nothing about this house. Kate went on crying. Leo Bailey stroked her shoulder. Gradually her cries diminished. Jessie began closing off the doors leading to the hall and bedrooms, furiously hammering metal strips at their sides, tops and bottoms. "We'll suffocate!" sobbed Kate. Jessie went on hammering.

"We may not suffocate," said Leo Bailey, "but if the house is hit, we'll be trapped in this room. With the pressure—the walls could cave in—"

Jessie stopped hammering. The house may be hit, she said, in an awesomely quiet voice, but it will stand. It's built on concrete, and it's on a twenty-foot cliff. I'm sealing off the outer rooms so we'll have a barrier on all sides. We're safer in this room than we would be anywhere else on the island. Just where did you think we might go, anyway?

"Into town," said Leo Bailey. "High ground up near the club. Collins Hill, where the church is."

Jessie laughed. Swim there? Now? She went back to her carpentry.

"Here," said Leo Bailey, "let me give you a hand."

Jessie tossed him a hammer, a box of nails and three strips of metal. Go do another one, she said tersely.

"Where are you taking the flashlight?" Kate asked. "We need it—"

We have two, said Jessie. One goes in Robin's room, facing the bay. And stays on—for Diane. In case—*when* she comes back.

Diane had been running along the water's edge, still shrieking for Robin to come too, when the first massive waves began washing over her feet. She kept trying to run, slipping and falling, until the water reached her knees. Then she stumbled across the rocks to the flooded roadbed of Ocean Drive. The waves pursued her. If she could reach a house, she thought, she could break a window and hide inside, until it was over. Unless it turned out to be the end of the world. But cottages on both sides of the road were breaking up and floating away. She clung to jutting rocks, ducking as parts of kitchen stoves and chimney tops flew past her; refrigerators and sofas; great chunks of wooden walls that might have been chewed off by some monstrous animal. Windows sailed above her head like transparent magic carpets. Her legs and feet were a mass of cuts from the sharp rocks she couldn't see under the swirling water. She was hit twice, once in the face, by flying shingles torn from housetops a mile away. She could not see them coming through the blinding spray and blowing sand. The sky was soon as filled with wreckage as the torrent surrounding her. And all of it, even the crashing of the waves and the breaking of buildings, was silent. Silent as a television war with the sound turned off. The high scream of the wind, Muzak piped into Hell, to drown out reports of local conditions.

Chapter 9

DESPITE ALL THE SPYING on Minerva, despite the brilliant, painstaking detective work at radar posts strung halfway across the continent, Minerva got away from them. At the last minute, she eluded the vigilant men who had been assigned to her case, trained to eavesdrop on her breathing, to analyze the rhythm of her sighs. She had run out on them; disappeared right from under their experienced noses. She did not wander far. In fact she barely wavered from the path she was expected to take. Not really flighty—just slightly out of control, or at least out of their control. During the last few hours of her wild western streak over the water on November 18, had she followed a course a hair's breadth to her right, as she had indicated, Andrea Island would have been spared. Dozens of other storms over half a century had traveled along her same general route without inflicting serious harm. But Minerva's impulsive rampage caused more chaos in those few hours than the historic storms of 1815, 1938 and the infamous, equally well monitored Carol of 1954. Only Camille's attack on the Gulf

Coast in 1969 and Agnes's in 1972 destroyed more millions' worth of property.

Some said Minerva's sudden furious surge into Andrea Island might actually have been caused by the human efforts that had been marshaled to divert her course or diminish her intensity. Possibly the experimental seeding had backfired and somehow increased her strength, or driven her wild. It had happened before.

There were different theories. The only hard fact was that the crazy loop she had taken, the sudden lurch forward, had confounded everyone. The whole world had known where she was and where she was going—except for the people directly in her final chosen path—yet she managed to strike without warning, with the supernatural force of the warlike goddess after whom they had naively named her. Minerva, who wore a breastplate emblazoned with the head of a Gorgon—a terror of the sea in female form.

The eye reached Andrea Island at 3:15 P.M., passing over bay and shore, still moving north. Suddenly the wind died, and the sun emerged in a brilliant blue sky. During that brief, eerie lull, many people were sure the storm had ended, and came out of hiding to look at the damage.

"Listen," cried Kate, "it's stopped." Jessie understood the silence. No, she said, it's barely begun. Leo Bailey nodded gravely. If it was the hurricane, then Jessie was right. Diane will know, said Jessie, as though she were willing it to be so. She paused and then said it again, with assurance: Diane will know.

They sat in the dark and waited for nearly an hour until the shrieking began again, louder and stronger than before. The eye had passed. Outside, the sky grew black again, and again rain fell. The wind abruptly shifted course, as if Minerva were turning back to see what she might have missed. With her second wind, she flew even faster and higher, with stronger gales from the rear half of her deadly ring now whirling in from the ocean. She flew at a hundred miles an hour, a hundred and ten, with gusts in some places as high as a hundred and fifty. The Waterman house shook and creaked. Rain was now hitting it horizontally, seeping through the thick outer walls. A chunk of ceiling fell near the dining room table. They heard a terrible crack below them. Garage door, said Jessie. I think it's blown off. Better put up the dining room table, she said to Leo Bailey. Just in case. They carried the heavy oak refectory table to the door leading downstairs, and nailed it up on top of the closet door and metal crossbars already there. The house groaned beneath them, as if it had shifted from its foundation. "The floor is sagging," Kate whispered. It will be all right, said Jessie. Under her breath she added, Diane—it will be all right. I promise.

Outside, the wind was rolling up the ocean like a giant rug. The storm wave, reaching up thirty to forty feet, was heading in to shore, where it would cover land, people and houses in a deadly fog-colored shroud.

The house did not cave in. Suddenly Kate began to giggle. "Tell me, Mr. Bailey," she said in an odd, high-pitched voice, "did the Coast Guard really have any idea this was coming?"

"*Some* idea," said Leo Bailey, with a nervous grin.

Kate giggled again and stretched out on the sofa, resting her head on Leo Bailey's lap. "Wake me when it's over," she said. Leo Bailey began to play with strands of her hair, as though they were rosary beads.

Robin, fully revived, wanted to know why they couldn't go out and find Diane. Jessie explained that Diane was all right, but that there was no way they could find her now.

"Then how do you know she's all right?" Robin persisted. I just *know*, said Jessie quietly. The way I know about the storm. Robin considered that, and then nodded, accepting it. "Can I play something, then?" she asked.

You can't get to the dolls now, said Jessie.

"Oh, I don't need them. There's cardboard and cups and stuff in the cupboard. I can use those."

Can you play in the dark? I'll need the flashlight, said Jessie. I have some writing to do.

Robin said she could set up her things near Jessie. She collected scissors, tape and glue, crayons and Jessie's staple gun.

Be careful with that, said Jessie. They moved to the small writing desk in the dining area, and Jessie began to write in her diary. From time to time she glanced toward the darkened living room. She saw Kate's head move slightly in Leo Bailey's lap; she saw it turn and burrow against him. She saw Leo Bailey's hands, buried in Kate's hair. They seemed to clasp Kate's head now, drawing it closer. She thought she saw . . . but they had scarcely shifted position. Perhaps she only imagined. In any case, she had not seen Kate's furtive glances in her direction, or Kate's secret smile.

Robin was constructing an elaborate landscape, a sea flecked with tiny sharp peaks, red, black and white. She murmured softly to herself as she worked. "What are you building?" Jessie asked.

"Atlantis," said Robin. "The lost island kingdom."

Jessie didn't hear her. She was still watching Kate's head and Leo Bailey's body.

I suppose it was inevitable, Jessie thought. Though I hadn't expected it quite so soon. I did know it would have to be faced some day, though, and that when it came I wouldn't be ready. How hard is it going to be, I wonder. She suddenly realized that she was afraid. Not so much of the coastguardsman as of the enemy within. If only she could think of that lurking demon as imaginary, a psychic anomaly, half a split person, a Hyde to save. But that was not what she was. Weak and dying, perhaps, but real. Jessie knew that she was still capable of regaining her strength and staging a last comeback. She had not quite, not yet, relinquished her rightful claim. Rightful; that was the threat. Jessie shook her head to clear it. She had to stop thinking this way or there would be no end to it. The memories . . . the reflexes. She would begin to feel the pressure again, the welling up; worst of all, the awful . . . weakness. Soft, pliant core that would yield, would give way. God, how it longed to soften and spread . . . Jessie could not let that happen now. Jessie swore she would hold her ground. *She* is no match for me, Jessie told herself. Never was. And if that was true, Jessie could find a way to break her—force her out. She would have to yield to Jessie. Now. Once and for all. Weaken and destroy. B. G. would understand.

Jessie switched off the flashlight and began sketching in the darkness. She let her hand guide itself over the drawing pad, freely, out of control. She drew a portrait of Coastguardsman Leo Bailey, nude and in profile, and next to it, a woman's head. The woman's eyes were half-closed, lost in a dream or ecstasy. The full lips were parted, as if she were about to speak or sigh, or . . . On the whole, the face resembled Kate Saville— that is, it had Kate's long dark hair, her eyes, her delicate pointed chin. Hoydenish. But the mouth—the parted mouth —was unmistakably Jessie's. In the lower righthand corner of the drawing, Jessie added an elaborate monogram signature. *Jessie* was written in small neat script, with a jagged line drawn through it. Underneath, in bold, sharp letters, she had written *B. G.*

. . . B. G. had caressed her breast with the gun. She had taken a black lover. Called it Roy and let it do with her what B. G. willed. How easily. How cocksure it had been, gliding in as if it lived there. As if Roy had come home. Something clicked into place. Roy had come home. Never mind, B. G. said. Leave it in. Let's show him how you do. He would see her like that, Roy would find her like that with the gun. Watch her explode. Ahh. B. G.'s laugh, short, a dog's barking. He said Roy could have a turn next. Only fair, he said. Roy could either use the gun or watch B. G. use it. Roy had a choice. Perhaps he couldn't choose. Down in the darkness, she had sighed, finally. Ahh. As if she didn't care what they decided.

At 4:45, Minerva lifted the spire of Holy Family Church on Collins Hill, and carried it off like a prize. At least two dozen Andrea Islanders, refugees of the storm, huddled in shelters on the high ground of Collins Hill, recalled later that they heard the bell tolling and then saw the steeple dashed to pieces at the bottom of the hill, some thirty feet from the church building. It was the only sound, other than Minerva's voice, that anyone heard throughout the storm's occupation of the island. Minerva's voice—an extraordinary minor chord composed of three pure notes: the low wild moaning of the sea, the high keening of the wind and, between and above them, her own dominant throbbing *ululu*, played on some magnificent organ, more felt than heard, a sound experienced by the whole body, like an orgasm, like the thrill of terror, like nothing one ever expected to survive.

According to official reports, the storm ended at 5:30, though brutal, lashing winds continued for several hours, and flooding for several days. On Ocean Drive only two structures were still standing—the old fort on the point, and the Watermans' house. All the other buildings—the beach club and cabanas, the yacht club, the Coast Guard tower and twenty-five summer cottages—had been demolished or washed into the bay. Some had gone when the first powerful waves hit the shore before the storm's climax, while Diane Waterman was still running along the flooded roadbed. The rest were swallowed up by the great rolling tongue of surf that leaked out of the sea after the wind shifted. La Ronde beach club split open, sending a shower of bar stools, Ping-Pong tables, pool umbrellas and a jukebox into the air like surprises from an exploding birthday cake.

Ocean Drive itself, the long, narrow finger of land that stretched out from the town's center to Andrea Point, had been severed from the main part of the island by a new inlet, carved by the storm through the beach, from ocean to bay, and filled with rushing water. It was as clean a cut as if it had been made by a knife.

"What's Atlantis, Robin?" Leo Bailey asked.

"It was this big island," Robin said, "near Greece. Disappeared one day, just like that. 'In one bad day and one bad night.' That's what Plato said."

"Then how does anyone know it was ever there? How did Plato know?"

"Some people said he made it up. But the Egyptians knew about it, too, and the Athenians. Some people think it was where Odysseus got shipwrecked. Anyway, it was real. It had a whole civilized culture, and stone walls, and a powerful army. There was a king's island, where they built a silver temple with gold spires. They had—"

"So what happened to it all?" said Leo Bailey. "How come nobody ever found anything?"

"They found things. Pieces of stone. Other stuff." She showed them her construction—the bleak seascape with barren cliffs jutting out of the water. "Pieces of Atlantis," she said. "And over here . . . this is Thera."

"The volcano? But that's all the way at the eastern end of the Mediterranean."

"Thera," said Robin firmly, "blew up and buried Atlantis. There was fire, and drought, and quakes and tidal waves. . . ."

"Were there any survivors?" asked Kate.

"I don't know," said Robin. "Anyway, I was just going to do the explosion. Enormous waves of water that buried whole villages hundreds of miles away. Tons of dust, millions of tons, and poisonous vapor. Crete was covered with it. All the fields, the cities. . . ."

"How do you know all that?" said Leo Bailey. "They teach that in school out here?"

Robin shrugged impatiently. "Books," she said. "Anyway,

106

that's when Crete stopped being powerful. Crete sort of just died. That was how Greece took over. And the sea people attacked Egypt. They got captured and they told why they had to become warlike. They said it was because their whole island was torn loose and carried away in a storm."

"It's a fascinating fairy tale," said Kate.

"It's not a fairy tale." Robin's eyes flashed. "It was just as real . . . as this is."

Jessie had been listening intently, but not to anyone in the room. It's over, she exclaimed suddenly. The wind was still blowing fiercely; trees were still falling. In the center of town, eight feet of water coursed through the streets, still rising. Rumors flew among the survivors that the island was sinking. Armed guards patrolled the shopping area. The library was set up as a morgue. Jessie got up and started stripping the metal supports off the door leading to the bedrooms. "Are you sure?" said Kate.

Sure, said Jessie. If Diane doesn't . . . I mean if she's stranded somewhere, it will be another whole day, at least, before we can go look for her. And I don't know if the house will survive the flooding. She paused, then added firmly, But it *is* over. She went to Robin's room to make sure the flashlight was still shining out toward the bay. Control it, she whispered. I know you can, Diane. I *know* you can.

Chapter 10

DIANE HAD BEEN WASHED into the bay, clinging to a telephone pole. The pelting rain of debris from wrecked houses fell all around her, sometimes striking her, sometimes missing. She could fend off some of it with her free arm, or duck under the water for safety. Finally a peaked section of someone's gray shingled roof floated past her, upside down. She let go of the pole and swam to it eagerly, crawling inside. Later she tranferred to a floating door, then a section of floor with an upright piece of broken pipe for a mast, and finally the front half of a broken rowboat. Once in the boat, she sailed—over the tops of trees and submerged houses, sunken cars and trucks. Like a child in a giant bath filled with bathtub toys. She sailed until her broken ark hit mud and would sail no more.

Then she crawled out, cautiously, up to her chest in water, still surrounded by wreckage, but touching earth with her feet. There was a tree, tall enough to have branches above the waterline—and she made her way to it. She could just reach the lowest branch and hoist herself up. She hung there, in the howling darkness, feet dangling, water up to her waist. It was about five o'clock in the afternoon. Diane was no more than two miles from home.

Jessie had gone to put Robin to bed. Kate took the flashlight from the dining area and brought it back to the living room. Before setting it down on the glass coffee table, she held it up close to Leo Bailey's face. "I've never really seen it," she explained. "Very young."

"Not so young," he replied defensively. "Twenty-two."

"Old enough to handle strange women in the dark, right?"

He laughed, embarrassed. "I guess so," he said. "Although it depends how strange."

Kate didn't laugh. "Does it happen often?"

"Not very. Most of the time they ask first."

"How civilized," said Kate. She paused, then added teasingly, "Maybe Jessie will ask."

Leo Bailey didn't know what to say to that, so he said nothing.

"Would you like that?" Kate asked.

He shrugged. "Hadn't thought about it."

"I thought about it," said Kate, "the minute you walked in."

"You did?" said Leo Bailey, startled. "I mean, about her asking—or you?"

"Her," said Kate airily. "I *knew* about me."

"Well," said Leo Bailey uncomfortably. "We'll all be here awhile, probably. So if she wants to ask, she'll have plenty of time."

"And you—don't you ever ask first?"

"No," said Leo Bailey. "I like to be surprised. Makes me feel attractive."

"Anybody ever surprise you by *not* asking, when you figured she would?"

"Once in a while, sure."

"What did you do?"

Leo Bailey cocked his head playfully. "You know," he said, "I forget."

Kate was standing in the hall when Jessie came out of Robin's room.

She all right? said Kate.

She's been all right all day, hasn't she?

Yes, said Kate defensively, but sometimes she's frightened for no reason. Seems to me tonight she had a reason.

True, said Jessie. But she's all right. She paused, then added, with only a hint of irony, I assume you are too?

Kate pretended not to hear the irony. Oh, n fine, she said brightly. What do you think of our Coast Guard?

Jessie started to walk away, toward her own room. She shrugged. Our Coast Guard serves its purpose, I imagine. There was a trace of emphasis on the word *our*.

Kate said, Like—a necessary evil, you mean?

Jessie sighed. I don't know, Kate.

But Kate followed her, into her room. Don't know if it's necessary? Or if it's evil? She reached out and touched Jessie's shoulder, lightly.

What are you trying to do, Kate? Test me?

Understand you, said Kate. She did not remove her hand. I thought we understood each other very well. Kate sighed and moved the hand to the back of Jessie's neck. They were standing very close now. Do you love me, Jessie? she murmured.

Say the magic word and all will be well? whispered Jessie. I can't. But she whispered it against Kate's mouth, with a kiss that Kate could find consoling. All I know is you're necessary to me, Jessie said. I can't imagine not—having you. Sweetness and measured fire. A true lover's kiss. Kate was trembling.

Is that how you think of me—as something you own?

As a person who belongs to me—yes. And to whom I belong. . . .

I don't feel that, murmured Kate. Not in the least.

Slowly Jessie opened the buttons of Kate's shirt. Slowly bent and kissed each of her breasts. Slowly, tenderly, took all of Kate into her mouth. Do you feel it now? she said. Now? Kate could not answer; that was her answer.

Jessie had won a crucial victory. She knew it the instant Kate began trembling in her arms. But there would be a price —she knew that too. The pressure had already begun. Pounding now, almost unbearable. She had expected it. She had known it would set off something. The violence, and the breasts—all at once. Had to have an effect on *her*. She would act up, try to break out. She would expose herself, confess— what? Her need, her crying need to be protected? God, Jessie thought, I don't *want* to protect her any more. Enough. I want to kill her. Close your eyes, Jessie . . . breathe . . . count . . . fantasy: Jessie and Kate. Jessie strong and sure, moving into Kate's body; Kate accepting, welcoming, trusting. Jessie opened her eyes and waited for the sense of exultation, knowing it would not come. The pressure grew more intense; racking. Even Kate felt the change in Jessie's body. What is it? she murmured. Jessie shook her head. No, she said, almost inaudibly. No. For an instant Kate saw Jessie's face as that of a lost, anxious woman—someone trying to please. She pulled away, bewildered.

In another minute Jessie felt the pressure begin to subside.

It's all right, she said to Kate. It was nothing. Come back here. Kate came back. Maybe, Jessie thought, feeling her strength come back, too, maybe it's just never going to happen. Maybe she can't be destroyed. Have to live with her forever. The essential tragic flaw, like the damage from a miserable childhood or a congenital heart defect. Something I can learn to compensate for. She pulled Kate gently toward the bed. Maybe that's the answer. *She* is the skeleton, and I am only the closet.

Jessie. . . ? Kate whispered.

I'm here, she answered smoothly, surely. My Kate. My own sweet Kate. I love you.

After Kate fell asleep in Jessie's bed, Jessie got up and began inspecting the house. She carefully removed a few boards from a few windows, and opened the sliding glass doors enough to let in some air. Then she went back to rejoin Leo Bailey in the living room. It was still raining quite hard, but the winds were gradually diminishing. Jessie sighed. "I still can't quite believe it's over," she said. "Diane's out of danger." Leo Bailey shook his head admiringly.

"Beats me," he said, "how you know so much about hurricanes. I know—you used to be one of those TV weather girls. Right?"

Jessie smiled politely. "I really *don't* know much about them—but I share some of their feelings. Sympathy for their cause, in a way. It gives one a certain—"

"Ah," said Leo Bailey, nodding. "Woman's intuition."

"If you like," said Jessie.

"Why do they give them girls' names, anyway?" asked Kate, from the doorway. Neither of them had seen her standing there. She came in and sat next to Leo Bailey, aiming one of her sly half-smiles at Jessie.

"I don't know," said Leo Bailey. "Used to name them for Spanish saints—of both sexes."

"Until they discovered they weren't saintly? No madonnas —all whores?" said Kate, laughing.

"I don't think—" said Leo Bailey uncomfortably.

"Probably started in World War II," said Jessie. "That's when they started giving everything women's names. Even fighter planes. . . ."

"Everything owned or operated by men, right?" said Kate.

"Everything," said Jessie, "except hurricanes."

Kate yawned. "Wonder if the Coast Guard has sent the rescue boats out yet for Surfman here."

"Take a day or two," said Leo Bailey. "Then they'll patrol the shoreline, picking up survivors. I imagine they'll find a fair number. Clinging to wreckage, or washed up on some of the little islets in North Bay."

"And the lucky ones who made it to houses that weren't hit," said Jessie.

Leo Bailey grinned. "The luckiest."

"Of course," said Kate, "this house could still collapse, couldn't it? I mean, it's sitting in water up to its armpits."

"Right. I may have to evacuate you after all," said Leo Bailey. "Although if we don't sink tonight, the water will probably start to recede. Assuming the rain stops by morning."

"Then I think we ought to celebrate our survival tonight," said Kate. She hesitated. "Jessie?"

A flicker of something crossed Jessie's face. It couldn't be fear, Kate thought. She seemed to be . . . deciding.

"All right," Jessie said finally. "Might as well use up the wine. If we go down tonight after all, it'll be too late."

Kate and Leo Bailey laughed; Jessie smiled at them absently, like an indulgent mother.

"Shall we light some candles and curse the darkness?" Kate asked.

"Not me," said Leo Bailey. "I'll never curse the darkness again. Too many good things happen in it."

"How do you know they're good," said Kate playfully, "if you never get a good look at them?"

Leo Bailey laughed again. "If they feel good, that's good enough. Unless I'm buying a used car." He winked at Kate.

"You sound very sure of yourself," Jessie murmured. She sipped her wine slowly. Kate and Leo Bailey drank fast and steadily. Jessie watched them refill their glasses twice. Then she began to refill them, and went to get another bottle. There was a lot of laughter—an air of relief, mingled with lingering anxiety and sexual tension. Kate sat very close to Leo Bailey, their thighs touching. Now and then Kate would lean toward him, or his arm would brush some part of her, possibly by accident. This time Jessie was not imagining.

"Hey, Surfman," Kate said suddenly. "Isn't Jessie beautiful?"

Leo Bailey stared into his wineglass. "You're both fine-

113

looking b— women," he mumbled. White lie, he thought, pleased with it. Kate was a sexy bitch. He wouldn't mind a little of that. The other one was peculiar, though. Something about the way she moved. Wouldn't want to mess with that one.

"Fine-looking b— women," Kate echoed, teasing. "You mean"—she lowered her voice to a conspiratorial whisper—"you'd like to, uh, with *both* of us?

"Is that what you'd like, Kate?" said Jessie in a low voice. Leo Bailey shifted uneasily on the sofa.

Kate giggled. "Maybe," she said, teasing. "Maybe. . . ."

"How about you and two men?" Jessie persisted. "Ever dream about being 'taken' by two strong men?"

"Sure," said Kate lightly. "I used to dream of being, of taking on a whole college fraternity. They kidnapped me and kept me locked up in one of the rooms. Then they'd take turns—two, three boys at a time. I was their initiation ceremony. I—"

"Did they hurt you, in the dream?" Jessie asked.

Ice, Leo Bailey thought. Dry ice. Maybe a lesbo.

"Well," said Kate, "they were rough. They tore my clothes. You know—and laughed a lot about what they were doing. Or what they wanted me—"

"I did that once," said Leo Bailey suddenly. "Me and three buddies—"

"You—you raped a girl?" said Kate, wide-eyed.

Leo Bailey looked startled. "We, you know, we were just fooling around. We didn't—I mean one of the other guys picked her up. She was ready to go with him. She just didn't count on four of us being in the car, that was all."

"That was all?" said Jessie.

He answered without looking at her. "Well, I mean, we drove around awhile. Till she quieted down. She was okay." What the hell, he thought, she's not the D.A. But his palms were sweaty. "She was okay," he said again, still not looking up from his wine.

"What do you mean, she quieted down?" Kate wanted to know. "Did you hit her—or just scare her, or what?"

"No, like I said, she got quiet after a while. Nobody hit her or anything. Just held her and told her we wouldn't hurt her any. Just drove around till she decided . . . till she said she was ready."

Kate's face was flushed, almost feverish. "Didn't she, didn't she cry—or anything?"

Leo Bailey shook his head. "Didn't make a sound. It was weird, the way she was so quiet."

"Well, what happened afterwards?" Kate said. "When you —when you were finished?"

Leo Bailey shrugged. "We just let her out of the car. She was okay . . . you know, what's really weird is talking about it. I mean to you. I never told anybody—"

"But weren't you afraid?" Jessie demanded. "Didn't you feel . . . guilty?" Her voice was tight and strained suddenly, but she had to do this. Had to understand how he felt.

"No," he said sharply, and then shrugged, as if to push the whole thing away. Push Jessie away, with that weird blue stare she had. Challenging.

Kate said, "Did you ever do it again? I mean with anyone else?"

Leo Bailey looked shocked. "Hell, *no*," he said defensively. "What do you think—"

"Why not?" Kate persisted. "Wasn't it—didn't you . . . like it?"

Leo Bailey hesitated. Okay, let them have it. "Well," he said, looking straight at Kate, "well, yeah. I mean, sure. I'd be lying if I didn't admit there was, that it was exciting. But it was, you know, kid stuff. Something you go along with, once, when you're a kid. Why not, you figure. But even then you know it's—that a man doesn't—that a man has to take his women alone, like anything else. A man has to—"

"So that's what you do now?" said Jessie. "Take your women alone?"

"I didn't mean it that way." He sounded indignant. "I don't 'take' anybody doesn't want taking. Like I said before, they—women—usually ask me first."

"That's right," said Kate, stifling a giggle. "That's just what he said before. I think it's adorable."

Jessie's eyes never left Leo Bailey's face. He couldn't figure it, what she wanted from him. Hated those eyes of hers, boring into him. Why couldn't he just tell her to back off? Change the subject. "Don't you still feel that you're doing the taking?" she demanded.

"Not every time," he muttered. "I don't know!" He didn't know; she was confusing him. What the *hell* did she want?

Jessie nodded thoughtfully. "If a woman is really in control, if *she's* using *you*—"

"Hell," said Leo Bailey, laughing suddenly. "That makes it better. Sexier. She *thinks* she's using me, but she's really setting herself up. Only she doesn't know it. Say she's got some kind of need for me, some other guy she's getting even with, or she's proving something to herself—that she's independent—liberated—she doesn't care who she—hell, it doesn't matter what she needs me *for*. Whatever it is, it's me she needs for it, so I got it made. She's right where I want her, and I didn't have to do a thing—it's beautiful." He reached over to squeeze Kate's arm for emphasis. It was a buddy's touch, conspiratorial. Kate moved away slightly, conscious of Jessie's eyes, of her own mounting excitement.

"Why is it beautiful?" said Jessie. "You're enemies."

"Who's enemies?" said Leo Bailey. "It's just the way you play the game. She wants to win something off me; I want to win something off her. It's—Christ, it's fun."

"Fun," echoed Jessie, tonelessly.

"Sure," said Leo Bailey.

"What if," said Kate, "you're the one who needs?"

"That happens," said Leo Bailey. "Want somebody real bad, and she knows it? I've been there. Begging, promising things. She feels strong, she can say no, or do me a favor. She

116

knows I'm weak then, I got to have her—and she's got the power. She can keep it up—maybe she'll do me the favor, maybe not, she'll think about it. Oh, yeah, I've been there."

"And you don't feel taken, feel screwed, when she . . . does you the favor?"

Leo Bailey laughed again. "You still don't get it," he said. "She gives in to me, then it's all turned around. I get all the power back, and then some. I got her to screw, don't you see? *I* screwed *her*, no matter what she thinks. I can cross her off then, walk out on her, or threaten to. I've had her. She can beg now, she can go 'But you said you loved me!' Sure, I said it, I'd say anything when I was begging. But then I won—"

"I still don't see," said Kate, "why you don't just skip all that and take her by force, the way you did the girl in the car, with your buddies. Why is that kid stuff, and what you're doing now being a man?"

"What are you, kidding me now?" said Leo Bailey.

"No," said Kate, "I mean it. If a woman is giving you trouble, don't you ever think of just . . . bulling your way—?"

"Well, sure," said Leo Bailey slowly, "I *think* about it."

"But you never do it?"

"Of course not. You can't just—"

Kate's sudden laugh was taunting, provocative. It went on too long, and that made Leo Bailey angry.

"Hey, what are you laughing at?" he said. "Me?"

"Stop it, Kate," said Jessie coldly.

"Aye, aye, sir," said Kate, through her laughter. "They say that in the Coast Guard—aye, aye, sir?"

Leo Bailey said nothing; he emptied another glass of wine. Jessie refilled it.

"I said stop teasing the man, Kate."

"I wasn't 'teasing,' " said Kate, annoyed.

"Being provocative, then. Deliberately provocative."

"And you—just what were you being? Asking him the complete Kinsey questionnaire? What was that all about?"

117

"I was—" Jessie began, and then changed her mind. "It's not the same thing at all, and you know it."

"Hah," said Kate. "You think *he* could tell the difference?"

"I think," said Jessie, "we should all get into some dry beds, before we start to say things we mean."

Leo Bailey was suddenly feeling the wine. He yawned. "Think I'll just stretch out right here, if—" and he was asleep.

Chapter 11

LEO BAILEY lay curled up in the fetal position, snoring loudly, when Jessie left Kate in her bed and returned to the living room. She stood next to the sofa, watching him, listening to the wind, weighing alternatives, and then reached an abrupt decision. The house would stand through the night. Tomorrow, she thought, they would have to go and search for Diane. And after that . . . So there was only tonight to do what had to be done.

The coastguardsman stirred in his sleep, flinging an arm out, the hand curled toward her in an almost childlike gesture of appeal. Jessie took it as a sign. She undressed quickly and lay beside him, curving her body against his. He stirred again, moaning. "Sssh," she whispered. "It's me, Kate."

Leo Bailey was very drunk. Jessie had made reasonably sure of that. Drunk, he would have no trouble providing what she wanted now. Or rather, what she required.

"Thought you'd wait up for me," she whispered, slurring the words slightly, to sound both drunk and Kate-like.

"Mmmf," he replied, with some effort. "Didn't know you were coming."

"Hey, Surfman," she said, blowing gently into his ear. "I need you to hurt me a little now. Think you could do that?"

"Huh? Why?" He started to turn toward her. She nudged him back gently, so that he couldn't see her too clearly. She had tied her hair up in a kerchief anyway, as a precaution. "Come on," she said, wheedling. "Pretend I'm the girl in the car that you—with your buddies. You know what I mean. Want you to—wouldn't you like to—that way?"

"Don't get it," he mumbled. "Want me to—?"

"Yes," she breathed. "Hard, and cold, and very fast. Want you to—"

She was getting to him. "Okay," he whispered, his voice thick. He could. If that was what the crazy cunt wanted, he certainly could. Rip her apart if she wanted.

"Harder!" she whispered. "Can't you—?" Taunting him with her breath. She bit her lip; he was hurting her now, tearing. Faster. She didn't want to feel the tearing. Just do it. She bit the lobe of his ear, hard, like a picador to get the bull mad. "Bitch," he rasped at her. Howled, and then attacked. He would . . . until she tore open beneath him, until he broke her like a cheap toy. That was how she wanted it. Yeah. Serve her right. He didn't know if she came or not; didn't feel her move. Sliding now, something oozing, blood and semen. He inhaled it like an intoxicant. Jesus. Jessie heard him groan, heard the ripping. Numb; cauterized. Then she too felt the wet, thick . . . stinging, she felt it stinging. Venom, she thought. Finally he lay back, exhausted. Jesus, he had really hurt her. She asked, he thought defensively; gave her what she asked. Crazy. Some women like that, hooked on pain, they want . . . punish them, some weird thing. Damn, he had never been so tired. His ear was bleeding, what the hell. That was the last thing she did; after that she hadn't fought him at all. No digging her nails into him, nothing. It was . . . he had to admit it was terrific. Must be a lot of freaks like that. He'd just never run into one before.

Funny thing, how all of a sudden he realized it wasn't Kate, but the other one, Jessie. No breasts at all, and that hard, angular body. Not that it mattered by then; by then it didn't matter who the hell she was. Still, he could have sworn she *said* it was Kate. And she called him something too. Or screamed it. Sounded like B. G. Some damn thing. That didn't matter either. All that he knew was how he felt, doing it to her like that. Hate-fucking her. Pure and simple—the purest and simplest. Just the way she wanted it, frozen stiff. Just what she came for. Damn. What he couldn't figure was why it was so great, the greatest. Better than anything he'd ever had. Even the one in the car. Hating and doing it like that, worse than anything you'd do to a whore, unless you were crazy. And whatever this one was, she was no whore. Better than just wanting it and getting it. It was something else, all right. Only one other thing in the world he could imagine would feel like this. Killing.

He thought again of the girl in the car, just a kid, that one, and his old buddies. He could see that girl's face now, white and scared under the makeup. Hot pink and dead white under the whizzing streetlamps. Fifteen, maybe. Don't hurt me, she had whined. I'll let you do it, I'll let you do anything, only. He had felt like a man then. Cooler than his buddies. The only one who could have given it to her all night. But this one was different. Jesus, it almost scared him. This one wanted, must have wanted him to *kill* her in there. Damn, that was it. Leo Bailey fell dead asleep, smiling, with his mouth pressed against Jessie's breast. She did not feel it. She felt only a sudden, overwhelming sense of release, of utter impenetrability. She would never again perceive the touching of her body, of her breasts, as an assault.

B. G., she said softly, swallowing the blood in her mouth. Don't leave me. Here I am, B. G.

B. G. caressed her breast with the gun, holding it there, ring of steel pressed to her nipple like a hungry mouth, nuzzling. And the nipple shrinking from it, erect with the coldness, fitting itself so, inside the barrel. Look at that, the way it just nosed right in. Adapting. B. G. laughed. Bang. He said that softly like a love word, burrowing into her. Gang bang. B. G. and company. Buddies. Call it Roy after your husband. After your husband has a turn. Fair enough; fair play. Roy could have used his own gun. No, man, she likes mine, B. G. had insisted. Look, man, look at that. They all like mine. Stop Roy, she had screamed. There was a sharp sudden sound, a bursting inside, something running red and black. B. G. had laughed. Jessie exploding red-black, red-black running down. Stop *Roy*. B. G. had laughed, voice like a dog barking Do it man, do it here I'll show you. And Roy would not stop, couldnotwouldnot. Come on, man, don't ever stop B. G. said nobody ever stops B. G. But it was Roy no don't come like that Roy *stop*. Roy had come, exploding laugh was that his laugh too, dog sound. Roy had come Ah, Jessie, Ahh, red-and-black, her blood and B. G.'s cock/gun Roy had come exploding finally Ah Jessie Ahh.

Chapter 12

DIANE HAD HUNG SUSPENDED from her tree branch, like a drip-dry rag doll, for nearly an hour, until the churning water subsided from waist level down to her dangling feet. Then she let go of the branch and climbed down. Dazed and shaking, she stood there for a minute, in freezing water up to her knees, and tried to think about what she was going to do if she was the only person alive on Andrea Island, which seemed very likely.

She could barely see; the whole ruined landscape still appeared to be enveloped in thick fog. She realized there was no way she could move, even if there were someplace to go. From the debris at her feet, she extracted a flat piece of wood without any nails sticking out of it, and propped it up against the base of her tree. Then she sat down in the water and leaned against the piece of wood, determined not to cry. She would wait here until something better occurred to her.

She waited there for ten hours. After a while, the rain stopped and the stars came out. It was a beautiful clear night, though Diane couldn't tell. The fog was in her own eyes; it was a blinding film of salt from the spray that had been whipping into her eyes all through the storm.

Now and then she would rouse herself by singing, or reciting her favorite Latin poems, practicing yoga postures, or getting up and flailing her arms at the sky, the tree, the emptiness. Things kept floating toward her and past her; she made them out dimly—remnants of other people's lives. A drowned kitten, a soggy pillow, part of a baby's crib. She stared at them through her stinging eyes and then looked away. Still, she wouldn't cry; there was no point. She thought of the old riddle about the tree falling in the forest. If Diane cries on an empty island at the end of the world . . .

Suddenly she wondered whether Robin was dead. Poor Robin, chasing after her toy assassins and her toy guillotine, might be the very last memory of a human being she would ever have. In spite of herself, Diane laughed out loud. If Diane laughs out loud on an empty island . . .

It was enough to make her feel better. She stood up again and stretched, yoga stretches, and then sat down to do the cross-legged positions. Maybe now that it doesn't matter any more, she thought, I'll be able to lower my knees perfectly to the ground. She had certainly never tried it while sitting in a foot of water, but for all she knew real yogis did it that way all the time. In any case, it was worth a try. Nothing to lose, she thought. That was funny, too.

She sat up very straight and placed her feet together in front of her, sole to sole, with exquisite care. If I do it, she thought, then it will mean that Jessie's alive and I'll see her again. Robin too, she added hastily, in case it might weigh anything in her favor. Okay, one, two . . . breathing deeply, exhaling slowly, she began to press her knees apart, lowering them. Gently now, like a flower opening; a yogic water lily. The knees floated wide apart, down and flat against the mud below the waterline. It was as if her hip joints had been released by a spring. Diane couldn't believe it. Hey, she yelled, into the darkness. Hey, everybody, *I can do it!*

Still yelling jubilantly, she glanced up at the sky and saw the stars. The salt film in her eyes had evaporated. Hey, she yelled again, hey it *worked.*

With that, she jumped out of the water and began to wade toward another clump of trees. Maybe there would be a road. Houses. Something to eat. People. Maybe she could get home, and it would still be there.

She wandered across a swamp and stumbled into ditches. She had no idea whether she was going in circles, or in a straight line to nowhere. She saw grotesque sights—trees whose leaves had been stripped off, leaving the bare stems still firmly attached to the branches. Dead birds whose feathers had been plucked clean by the wind. Shoes and clothing draped whimsically over twisted telephone poles, as if someone had put them out to dry, though there wasn't a trace of their owners, or their owners' houses. She saw a sailboat with a bathtub in it, and an upside down truck with a kitchen stove balanced upright on top of it. There was even a coffee pot on the stove. She saw the bodies of a drowned baby, a drowned wirehaired terrier and a drowned man in a raincoat and hip boots, with a broken umbrella clutched in his hand. But she didn't see anything alive.

Maybe, she began to think, she had been right the first time —she was the only one left. Don't be silly, she told herself firmly, remembering the yoga magic, and the stars. It had to mean something. She reached an open field and began to run. Please, somebody, be alive. Please, Jessie. . . .

Shortly before dawn Robin had such an intense dream that she woke up trembling with excitement. "Hatshepsut!" she whispered, climbing out of bed and racing to her doll closet. "Hatshepsut, of course." She was shivering with cold, but she wasn't aware of it.

Robin had a doll for every queen who ever ruled. But Hatshepsut was the only one who ever ruled as king. During her lifetime no one had dared challenge her claim to the title.

In her sleep Robin had heard the voice of Hatshepsut. Heard it say distinctly, in a foreign accent and a deep melodic tone, "Came forth the king of gods Amun-Re from his temple saying welcome, my daughter, my favorite, the king . . . *Hatshepsut, thou art king,* taking possession . . ."

Robin rummaged furiously in the dark closet for Hatshepsut's things—her ceremonial clothes, her magnificent temple, the tiny vials of sacred perfume . . . eye paint! Galena for the upper lids, malachite for the lower. . . . Why wasn't anything where it belonged, where she remembered it? Robin, usually so precise and methodical, knocked over boxes in her haste. Tomorrow she would have to reorganize everything. This was chaos. Boy, if Diane had been messing around in here, she would—Robin bit her lip. Diane might be . . . ah, there it was, the temple at Deir el-Bahri. She held it reverently on her fingertips. Dazzling creation. She had constructed the model a year ago—weeks of painstaking work, copying every superb detail, down to the interior wall paintings, from art-book color plates. She had even used a magnifying glass to decipher the hieroglyphs on the cartouches, before she found out that Hatshepsut's successor, her slimy stepson Thutmose III (Robin called him Titnose the Turd), had hacked off Hatshepsut's name everywhere it appeared, and stuck in his own name, so that no one would remember her. As if she never existed, much less reigned brilliantly for twenty years. As if she hadn't designed this whole temple herself, every glorious stone of it. Not that the historians admitted that, of course. Must have been Senmut's work, they said. Oh, sure, must have been old Senmut. The queen probably had an affair with him. Robin was positive that was a bunch of lies. Neither Senmut nor any other man in ancient Egypt had ever designed anything remotely like Hatshepsut's temple.

Robin held up her fragile monument to catch the sliver of

moonlight shining through her strip of open window. Its walls shimmered; Robin stared, awestruck, at her own handiwork. In this light none of the spilled glue or the blurry felt-tip markings showed. Only the magic.

Hatshepsut's painted eyes seemed to glisten, too, as if they sensed the importance of the occasion. Robin peered at the doll critically; her makeup seemed to lack something. She would have to come back to that. First she wanted to erect the giant obelisks. They were still lashed to the great raft Hatshepsut had had built to carry them from the Elephantine quarries. The infamous raft, for which she had ordered every sacred sycamore tree in the kingdom cut down. That was one of Robin's favorite scenes. "But your Majesty can't do that!" the viziers protested. "What about the figs? The people will have no figs!"

Robin would frown, as Hatshepsut had frowned her painted kingly frown. "You dare to think I give a fig about that?" she shouted. "The King must have the biggest raft in the world for her obelisks. Now start cutting those trees or I'll start cutting something else around here." Hatshepsut the king did not fool around.

Robin worked quickly now, untying the great obelisks and erecting them in place. There. She felt for the matches she kept hidden in Hatshepsut's ceremonial headdress. It was time to cense and perfume the temple for Hatshepsut's announcement.

She had served long enough as co-regent with her young stepson, ruling wisely, accumulating wealth and undertaking daring ventures. Egypt was at peace; her court was brilliant; everyone said that the queen had a will of iron, behind her beautiful face. Now it was time to claim her rightful title— all her titles. Well, maybe she would skip "Mighty Bull."

Robin lit the incense tapers. The fragrance of the gods filled the temple.

"Came forth the king of gods Amun-Re from his temple . . ." Robin intoned. She paused and glanced again at Hatshepsut's face. Something . . . but the eyes were perfect, and the elaborate headdress. She was impeccably attired in the robes of a king. Suddenly Robin remembered what it was. Hatshepsut had actually appeared before her subjects ritually bearded, as befitted a king. It was the final, spectacularly bold touch. Shocking. Historic. Solemnly, Robin fashioned the pointed beard out of cardboard, and affixed it to the doll's delicate chin. "There." Hatshepsut's eyes glittered again in the flickering light of the incense taper. Robin bowed her head, as Egypt had. Hatshepsut, thou *art* king, she whispered, taking possession of the lands.

Chapter 13

B. G. WOULD HAVE to come in from outside. Slip in through the narrow opening of the sliding glass door. He would like the feel of that, the tightness squeezing him. He would like the feel of the curtain too—light, gauzy, slightly damp—brushing against his body as he eased inside.

He made himself very straight, tensing and pushing in head first, with his shoulders hunched up. That was how he wanted to get in, the hard way, head first, just twisting a little back and forth because the opening was so tight. But he kept his hands pressed down at his sides. He would not use his hands or bend his body; he had to go in straight.

The rest would come easy, once he was inside. First he would stand still for a minute, breathing. Inhaling the darkness. He knew he would have to wait for the excitement to subside. What if it didn't? What if just . . . getting in like that . . . was so beautiful that it made him weak? He would just be standing there perfectly still, letting it wash over him, making him dizzy with the warmth of it. He knew he could not let that happen. He would have to run away then, pull out; he couldn't stand that, the shame of it. It was absolutely essential that he do it right, the whole thing, just right. Controlled. Like a man. He could do it; he would control the trembling. He would not let himself go. The trick was to stand there just long enough to get used to the feel of it, and the smell. Forcing himself to get over the rush of excitement, and to hold on to his strength. Feel it come back, coursing through his body like new blood. That would make the excitement die down enough so hc could control it. Enough so he could go on with the taking. Go on and take . . . something of the woman to prove . . . That was what he would need the gun for, to help him do it. The gun under the pillow. And then the excitement would come back, he knew this time it would come, high and clear and strong, singing like a scream inside him.

When it was over, he would think about a warm bath and something to eat, maybe, something wet and sweet that would slide down easily. Vanilla. He would think about lying in the warm tub and closing his eyes and listening to the water lapping at him. And it would be almost like getting in there again, feeling strong and straight as he moved inside, with the soft curtain brushing him, and the woman for him to take. After this, no one could say he wasn't a man.

Diane had been running hard for ten minutes when she stubbed her toe on a rock and slipped into a deep hole. She got up at once, thinking, If Diane yelled ouch on an empty island . . . but it hurt too much. So did her ankle, which had twisted under her when she fell. There was still no sign of a road, or a house. Nothing. Oh, what's the use? Diane cried angrily. Everybody thinks I'm dead by now anyway. She was about to sit down right there and give in to the tears, finally, when she spotted something bright out of the corner of her eye. She squinted. Small orange boat; one of those inflatable rubber things; a canoe. Lying on its side, about halfway between the clump of trees where she had started running and where she was now. Couldn't be more than a hundred yards from the spot where she had first landed all those hours ago. Don't get excited, she told herself sternly. The bottom probably has a hole in it. The thing is full of water. Maybe it's not a *big* hole. Maybe you wouldn't *find* the hole until you sank. And there's no paddle. Up the creek without a paddle.

Nevertheless she began to run toward it, ignoring the stabbing pain in her foot. The boat was full of water, but it wasn't torn. She turned it on its side to spill the water out, and examined it carefully, running her fingers over it anxiously as if it were an injured baby. Where does it hurt? Does it hurt anywhere? Here? *Here?* It was perfect. Paddle, she thought. Paddle? Her mind was racing. Something long enough to be a double paddle, because the boat is so light, and the bay's swarming with wreckage. She began picking furiously through the debris. Pieces of wood of every conceivable size and shape, but all flat and bristling with nails or splinters. Impossible. She couldn't even get her hands around them.

Oh, help, she thought desperately. Jessie, help. Diana, my goddess. Somebody. She was at the edge of the bay, still carrying the boat. What good are you? she said to it. Big fat useless . . . I might as well be back up in that tree. Tree . . . ? If she could hack off one of those branches somehow, it just might . . . like a long pole. She could wrap her sweater around the middle of it to protect her hands. But how do you hack off a branch? With a broken shingle? Flat rock? Bare hands? She began hacking.

It took a long time. Her shoulders were aching now, almost enough to make her forget the foot. Almost. But she had her pole. She waded carefully into the bay, holding the boat high over her head until she was out, chest-deep in water, beyond the fringe of wreckage. Then she lowered it gently into the water and climbed in.

She would hug the shoreline, as close as she safely could, threading her way slowly through the endless rushing stream of hazardous objects. Straining her eyes for a light, a telephone pole, a dock, anything. She had no idea how far she had to go, how long it would take. Only that this must be the way she had come, and that if she followed the shoreline it must lead her back. She had no doubt any more that she would get there, though the unending blackness along the shore kept reminding her that there might be nothing left to find. *Jessie. . . . Don't think about that*, she commanded herself sharply. She was moving, working the crude double paddle on one side and then the other, pushing things away from her boat. Things, bodies. *Don't close your eyes, one puncture and the royal barge deflates like an old birthday balloon, along with your last hope.* Blisters were forming on her palms and fingers. She felt them open and bleed. Her shoulders and arms were numb with weariness. The injured foot throbbed like a drum. *I am a wreck,* she thought. *Am I more of a flotsam or a jetsam? I think jetsam. It sounds like it's falling apart faster.* She paddled hard for another five minutes before allowing herself to pause and look back. *How far have I gone? Very far.* She couldn't see her tree any more. She looked up at the stars again, savoring the second good moment of the worst day of her life. She would remember. First, getting her knees all the way down. And then floating through the dark in a perfect inflatable boat with the best double paddle money couldn't buy. There was a third thing, she realized suddenly. She had stopped being afraid.

Kate only whimpered a little when B. G. said what he was going to do. But she jumped when he touched her, and he thought at first she might scream. He had to cover her mouth with his hand. Then he reached under the pillow for the gun. Slid the point of it inside her shirt and flicked it upward so that the shirt fell away; he could hear it tear. He was still covering her mouth with his hand, but he felt her body go limp. He knew she would not scream now. . . .

He laid the gun on its side against her naked belly and held it there for an instant until he could see her skin react to it. Then he began stroking her. He knew exactly what to do. Gently turning the thing back and forth to follow the curve of her flesh. Feel her heat rising, warming to it. Turn the mouth of it toward her and press it against her, like a kiss. Kate's eyes followed all its sinuous movements as though she were hypnotized. He slid it slowly down until it reached her groin, and then pressed the barrel against her there, hard. Inside, he said softly. All the way in. That was when she started whimpering again. No, she pleaded. No. But all he had to do was nudge her a little with it, and she went down the way he wanted her to. He stood for a moment astride her body, just looking down at her. Beautiful. God. Beautiful.

Where's your boyfriend? he demanded.

I don't have one.

Got a man there, in the living room, don't you?

Yes, but he's not—

Call him, said B. G. Hurry up. He backed away from her and opened the door. Don't move; just call him. Loud enough so he hears you. Not loud enough so anyone else does.

Surfman! Kate called in a ragged little voice. It was so easy, B. G. thought. Surfman!

After a minute, the shape of Leo Bailey loomed in the open doorway. Groggy. You all right, Kate? Thought I heard—

Come on in, Surfman, said B. G., pressing the gun to Leo Bailey's ear.

Who—?

Don't matter who, said B. G. Just get in here. He kicked the door shut behind Leo Bailey.

Kate moved slightly on the floor, but she said nothing.

Hey— said Leo Bailey. The butt of B. G.'s gun replied swiftly, with stunning precision, against his temple. That'd be the last warning, said B. G. quietly. Leo Bailey touched his head; it was bleeding heavily.

Now, said B. G. slowly, we have a better understanding. He explained to Leo Bailey what he intended to do to Kate. And when I'm through, he said, I count ten, not too fast. I get to ten, Surfman, and you're out. You're about halfway to town, I figure. They looking for you in the town, man, you suppose to help *rescue* people.

But— said Leo Bailey.

Ain't no *but*, man, said B. G. I count ten, just like a referee. Nine, ten, out. He smiled. Unless you just wash away in the tide. Lotta people did that today, right? Just washed away in the tide. You like to be missing in action, man?

Kate made another small noise. Shut that, said B. G. She stopped at once. Now, said B. G., what's your name, Surfman?

Bailey, said Leo Bailey.

Okay, Surfman, you just hold this for me here—hold her nice and steady for me—because my friend and I get kind of excited, times like these. You do know how that is, don't you, Surfman? B. G. laughed.

Leo Bailey said nothing. He did what he was told.

When B. G. finished, he held the gun to Leo Bailey's face. Clean it for me, Surfman. Leo Bailey did that too.

B. G. was satisfied.

Leo Bailey got his instructions. He was to report to the storm headquarters in town, explaining that he had been checking houses along Ocean Drive since the collapse of his watchtower. He was to say nothing about finding the Waterman house occupied. Nobody in here, said B. G. again, understand? Leo Bailey did not answer. Raped women, said B. G. thoughtfully. Hear we got a *surfman* went and raped women during this bad storm here. Name of Bailey. You understand now, boy?

Leo Bailey nodded. B. G. backed toward the door and opened it again. I'm going to start counting now, he said. Front door's unlocked. Don't want to see you again. Don't want to see no rescue boat in this area for twenty-four hours. This area is evacuated, far as you know. You searched it.

But— said Leo Bailey.

One, said B. G. Two. . . . Leo Bailey began running.

Diane had lost speed. Worse than that, she was in danger of losing control of the boat. She could no longer navigate well against the strong current, the pain and the fatigue. Both palms were raw and swollen from gripping the wet pole. The exertion of any extra pressure made her cry out. Yet without the pressure the light boat zigzagged crazily off course, requiring harder paddling to bring it back. Twice she had almost fallen asleep, her head dropping to her chest, her fingers loosening their grip. The pole began to slide into the water.

Better stop, she thought, despairing. Pull in to shore and rest awhile. Maybe just until it gets a little lighter. She felt as if it had been the middle of the night for three days.

Then too there was the nagging suspicion that she might have already paddled past the house, if there still was a house. She had seen nothing on the shore, not the hulk of a single building, not a tree. Things were still thumping against the boat. A swarm of live rats—she had been almost glad to see them, creatures still scurrying for their lives, just as she was. Another thump. Small bright bobbing object with a pale bit of cloth billowing around it like a sail. Tiny arms and legs pumping up and down, as if it were swimming. She reached out with the pole and hooked the end of it under the puffy material; fished the thing out and plopped it into the boat. Someone's broken doll.

She pulled the ragged, sopping dress down over its legs and straightened the bodice. The head was missing—sheared off. Charlotte! Diane cried. Dearest, dearest Charlotte Corday. She hugged the thing to her as though it were a beloved pet, a baby sister, saved from drowning. As though she would die if anyone harmed it. Charlotte Corday, whose execution she had attended only yesterday, cheering lustily as the blade fell. Oh, Charlotte, Diane crooned, will you be my best friend? And when we get home . . .

Chapter 14

THEY HAD LEFT KATE alone in Jessie's room. B. G. had disappeared the same way he had come. Leo Bailey's figure was retreating down the roadway—slipping, splashing, melting into the darkness. Kate got up from the floor and crawled into Jessie's bed. She needed to lie perfectly still, letting B. G.'s black silhouette imprint itself inside her closed eyes. She knew, or thought she knew, what he was, and why he had come. He hadn't really hurt her much. She sensed that he had deliberately held back—though he didn't seem reluctant to use force with the coastguardsman. It occurred to her that he might have been easier to hate now if he had hurt her more. Maybe that was why he hadn't. Not that the intensity of her hatred would make any difference between them. His power to hurt her, whether he used it or not, was all that he had needed to demonstrate. She had never been forced to confront her visceral response to that kind of power. He had come to make her do that; make her body admit what they both knew it felt. And he had succeeded. That was much worse than brutality or humiliation. No wonder he had taken such infinite pains not to injure her body. It would have distracted her from the real lesson.

As for the weapon, she understood that too. His power had less to do with the gun he was using than with her reaction to it. Her repulsion, her rage, her hostility. He had made her see that they were all his weapons, not hers. He had used them all against her. Suddenly she felt more terrified than when he had stood over her, looking down at her, murmuring, Beautiful . . . beautiful. A dreadful bond had formed between them at that moment. And now she would have to acknowledge it. Have to struggle against it. She would spend her life trying to destroy it. That made her his victim more surely than anything he could have done to her himself. Or might ever do. No, you don't, she thought defiantly. Damned if she would give in to that, let him . . . infect her like this, take over. She would resist him if it killed her. She'd resisted dominant men before. Roy Waterman—masterful old Roy Waterman. She hadn't let *him* get her. She'd used him. At least it seemed to her she had. She wasn't sure, now. She wasn't sure of anything now. The ground had shifted under her. Jessie had shifted it. Now, this . . . B. G. The worst of it was that it made her feel strangely light and free—dangerously so. Like a drug. Knowing full well there was nothing free about it—that it was a trap. Remember what Jessie said about the trap . . . seductive woman with hidden teeth. Hidden pointed objects, like guns. Like . . . No, you don't.

She was going to fight for her life—damned if she wasn't. She would leave this place; go back to the city—the civilized world. B. G. wouldn't dare follow her. But I've got to leave now, she thought, right now . . . or I'm hooked.

With Hatshepsut in her arms, Robin was gazing out her window, watching a veil of wispy clouds drift across the face of the moon. In the new brightness, she thought she saw an orange boat gliding over the water, close to the rocks below the house. On an impulse, she grabbed the flashlight and poked it through the narrow opening, as far as her arm would reach. She swung the light up and down, up and down. Maybe she should call out. What to say, though? Finally she yelled, *"Halt!* Who goes there?" That sounded right.

Diane heard the small voice before she saw the light. "Robin?" she whispered. *"Robin!"* she shrieked.

The pale ribbon of light rose and fell, breaking up in the choppy water. "Who *goes* there?" the voice challenged.

"It's me! It's—" Diane stood up in the boat and almost toppled out. *"Ro-bin!"*

Startled, Robin dropped the flashlight. It tumbled out of sight into the rocks, and went out. "Diane!" she wailed. "I dropped—wait, I'll—Diane, don't *move.* You hear me—? Stay right there!"

Diane nodded her head vigorously, and then started to laugh. She can't see me. If Diane nods her head in a canoe where no one . . . Suddenly her body began to shake uncontrollably, and the laughter became a series of violent sobs— spasms. Dry, choking spasms. The boat shook as if it were part of her, an extension of her; as if it would burst apart with her. Somehow she managed to jab her pole straight down through the wreckage, anchoring it in the mud. Planting it like a territorial flag. Then her head sank to her knees, and she sat there sobbing and shaking like a lost child. "Jessie," she sobbed. "Jess . . . *eee."*

She was almost unrecognizable. One eye was black, and the short, curly hair, matted with dried blood, stood out from her head like corkscrews of dark lightning. The injured foot was badly swollen and discolored; she had apparently broken the toe. Bare arms and legs, stiff and blue with cold; mouth white and caked with salt; fingers like swollen white sausages. Jessie wrapped her in blankets and held her on her lap, rocking her like an infant. She kept trying to tell them . . . jumbled images, like a disjointed nightmare. ". . . got my knees down, flat," she said, "in the mud." Then she would cry because no one understood that that was the good part.

Ssh, Jessie soothed. Tell us tomorrow. Rest now.

It seemed to calm her a little. She put her arms around Jessie's neck, nestling. So brave, Jessie murmured, massaging the cold arms. So proud of you. I knew you could. I knew. *Heroic.*

Robin sat quietly on the floor near them, rocking what was left of the other survivor, Charlotte Corday. Tomorrow Robin would find a new head to attach. Charlotte had been heroic, too. Again. She would never ever execute Charlotte again, no matter what Diane said.

Kate watched them all with growing discomfort, not wanting to acknowledge the cause of it. I am *not* jealous, she told herself; that's insane. But why couldn't I have been the one washed away and miraculously returned, if it would bring this much tenderness from Jessie? She was never like that with me, Kate thought. Never, not once. And now it's too late. Diane's one good eye peeked at Kate over Jessie's shoulder. Kate quickly averted her gaze. "Jessie," she said, rather too loudly, "don't you think we ought to let the child get some rest, in her own bed?"

Something in Kate's tone made Jessie stop rocking. She stared at Kate until Kate shuddered, an almost imperceptible shudder. Then Jessie smoothed Diane's hair back and kissed the bump on the child's forehead. Feel like going to bed? she said. Diane shook her head and buried her face against Jessie's chest, hugging her tighter. All right, Jessie said.

Kate's mouth tightened, too. She got up abruptly and marched to the door. "Is it okay, then," she said frostily, "if I use your room, Jessie? My bed is still soaked." Jessie nodded without looking up.

". . . here, right here," Diane murmured. Her body began to shake again. Kate shut the door behind her. It was not quite a slam, but almost.

Jessie caressed the sleeping child absently. It would be light soon; she would have to start making final plans. In the village, she knew, they would be setting up disaster relief committees, rescue squads. Boats would be launched. The Red Cross, working with telephone company maps, town registries, real estate agencies, would compile lists of the missing and unaccounted for. Survivors would identify the dead bodies washing up on the mainland. It would take just a little longer to comb the smaller islets at the far end of North Bay.

In a very few hours the town would be crawling with press and television cameras. The seven o'clock news would have a full hurricane wrap-up. Gaunt survivors streaming through the flooded streets, threading their way among fallen trees as though through a tropical rain forest. Solemn-faced volunteers shaking their heads. No, I'm sorry sir, no one by that name has turned up yet. We'll notify you if . . .

The news would make the European papers, splashed across the bottom of page one, with dramatic telephotos. Roy would try to call from Copenhagen or Vienna, just to make sure they were all right. The operator would tell him telephone service on the island was still disrupted, though it was expected to be restored within a few days. He would be connected to disaster relief headquarters in the nearest city; they had an emergency hookup. He would hold, thank you.

There would be a tight, sympathetic voice saying yes, sir, I'll try to help you what was the name sir would you spell that please.

No, sir, I'm sorry, no record as yet of anyone named W-a-t-e-r-m-a-n. Wife and two daughters? We'd better have a description, sir, ages, so forth. Ocean Drive, I've got that, yes sir, rented from whom? Yes sir, I have it now, we'll check . . . no sir, the school had been closed, 'count of the flooding.

. . . I'm sorry sir there doesn't seem to be a thing I can tell you at the moment. I've checked all . . . and there is this report on that area, states zero occupants found there during the storm. Was it possible Mrs. Waterman went into the city prior—staying with friends, perhaps? Not possible, Roy would say tersely. Jessie smiled, imagining his expression.

Well sir we'll just have to check it again and contact you if . . . yes sir the report was based on an actual Coast Guard search of the area. . . . The voice would have a slight crispness to it now. Coastguardsman stationed directly *in* the area at the time, sir, was able to check every house that hadn't . . . yes many of those houses were destroyed. No sir I'm not sure whether that one. Look, Mr. Waterman, I've already put a call in. Yes we do have boats in that area despite the report, of course sir. Always possible. In any case I'm sure we'll . . . yes sir we'll get back to you in a few hours, I understand of course, either way.

Jessie had been studying local maps and guidebooks even before the storm arrived. She had already considered the possibility of going . . . uninhabited islet somewhere. Hard on the children though—no school, no electricity. Unnecessary. Besides, too noticeable. One solitary family from nowhere suddenly materializing on an island that used to be empty. Must be something less risky. There was another spot though, smaller than Andrea Island, just a few miles out in North Bay. Reef Island. Jessie had hoped to find out more about it, but there wasn't time now. All she knew, from the guidebooks, was that it was a much poorer community than Andrea Island. No tourists, no summer people. Just a small colony of scallop fishermen, maybe a few hardy artists. Shacks probably demolished in the storm. B. G. would have to apply for a disaster loan, find a small house and an old boat. Local village boards would be helpful . . . small grant, maybe, for a family whose livelihood had been wiped out. Just might work. B. G. and family just might make it in a place like that, at a time like this. . . .

A shack and a small boat. Peace. B. G. might even take up painting again.

The only catch—the only failure—was Kate. Jessie realized now, too late, that it had been a mistake to assume Kate was ready for B. G., ready for him to change her life. What was more surprising was how B. G. felt about losing her. That he should care so much more than he had expected. And yet that Kate herself was not really the source of his pain. It was the failure that tormented him; the certainty that Kate had somehow slipped beyond his control, out of his territory. What he could not bear was the specter of Kate free of him, lost to him.

There would be others, of course. And in the meantime the children would exert their demands. Diane was still a child, in spite of her strength and spirit, in spite of the signs that she was already growing into a remarkable woman. There would come a time when she was far more of a woman than Kate. But not now. There were things Diane was not prepared for— things that B. G. could not prepare her for. There had to be someone to help with that—a Kate of some kind. A Kate, but not this one. There was no way to guess what would become of this Kate now. Or to accept the fact that B. G. would never know.

Diane stirred in Jessie's lap. Time is it? she mumbled. Almost time, said Jessie.

You sleep, Kate?

Kate hesitated. No.

Feel like talking a minute?

If you want to. Kate sat up. Jessie reached for her hand and held it. We have to go, she said gently. Matter of hours. The house—

You mean it's collapsing? Kate's voice had a tinge of panic.

We still have time. Jessie touched Kate's shoulder to reassure her. Her fingers stayed, resting lightly. I promise, she said.

But what about—I mean Diane's in no condition—

Don't worry, said Jessie, leaning forward. It will be all right. Let me lie down next to you, Kate. I need—

Kate looked at her guardedly. Don't look like that, Jessie said. I just need to hold you a little, it'll make this easier, what I have to say.

Kate leaned back tentatively, propped on one elbow as if she were ready to spring. Jessie put her arms around her. I want to tell you about B. G., she said.

I don't want to hear, said Kate. I hate him—

Don't, said Jessie, as if Kate had struck her. Accept him. He—

I hate violence, Kate said vehemently. I hate being used and frightened. That's all he's about.

Jessie's throat ached; she had to force her voice to cover it. He needs you, Kate, she whispered. He'd die to protect you.

From everything but himself, Kate said bitterly.

You belong to him, Kate, said Jessie. I swear you do.

It's not true, Kate protested.

Sure?

Of course I'm sure. She was not, though. She would never be sure.

There was a long silence. Well, said Jessie, finally. He won't push it. He'll survive.

They all do, said Kate.

It wouldn't work anyway, Jessie went on, if you didn't want to be there.

Be where?

Wherever he goes, said Jessie. He has to go somewhere, you know.

Kate looked at Jessie curiously. You mean he's going now? Right now? Does he know where? For how long?

Jessie shrugged. Some other little island, I guess.

Not back to the city? Ever?

Fish out of water, said Jessie, with a small wry smile. He belongs out here now. He always did.

Will he—what about the—Robin? And Diane?

Jessie didn't answer. Her lips brushed against Kate's face,

lingered at the edge of her mouth. Then she drew in her breath sharply and got up to go. Kate reached out to pull her back. Stay—

I can't, said Jessie. Something final about the way she said it. Dead. Kate did not protest.

Better get dressed then, Jessie said. I'll take you into town, to the . . . disaster relief center. They'll get you out of here by tomorrow. There'll be buses. The main roads will be cleared. Maybe even planes flying into the city. If that's what you want.

Jessie—? Kate said suddenly. What about, when Roy asks me?

Roy, Jessie said, pronouncing it as if it were a foreign word she would have to look up later. Oh, of course. You went home—when was it? Day before the storm. Last weekend. That was the last you saw of Jessie.

Kate stared at her in disbelief. You mean you're just going to disappear? With his children? Diane isn't even—I mean she has a *mother*—in California. You can't simply—

Jessie said again, You went home before it happened, Kate. You don't know anything else. She said it slowly; there was an ominous undertone.

But that's *kidnapping*, Jessie. I can't—

Sure you can, said Jessie evenly. And you will.

Kate fell silent, weighing that. I *have* to tell Roy, she thought. Roy has a right to know. At least that they're alive. Then she thought about it some more—Roy's right to know. How far that might extend. Jessie's eyes were watching her. Those damned blue-black eyes. She couldn't see the color in the dark. But she felt them change, felt the air change. B. G.—her body tensed. She would always feel this fearful tension—as if B. G. were holding her. Not loving, stronger than loving. Tears sprang to her eyes. She heard B. G.'s voice whispering in the dark. I don't study about love, baby. I just know what I got to have to make it. It's a natural thing. You know it is, you got it written in you, right down there. All written out in colors, and it lights up. Can't turn that off, no way. You afraid what it says, is all.

Kate was crying now. She felt as if her whole body were crying. Like Diane. You were all fine, she whispered, when I left. Before the storm. She looked up at the shadowy figure looming over her. The police will question me, won't they?

Don't sweat it, baby. You got no information.

I'll never see you again, Kate blurted suddenly. Jessie—

There was no answer.

Chapter 15

THE ONLY THINGS Diane cared about taking were her dreadful silver shoes, her notebooks and her Latin-English, English-Latin dictionary. Robin, on the other hand, wanted to take her entire doll collection, and the index file, along with all the elaborate sets she had constructed for her historical pageants. Jessie pointed out that the orange canoe was a two-person boat; the three of them would barely have room for a box of dried fruit and a jug of water. I don't care, Robin cried. Hatshepsut's not going without her temple, and I'm not going without Hatshepsut.

Jessie had told them only that the house was collapsing and in imminent danger of caving in; nothing more. Nothing about where they were going. She had expected a torrent of questions, but they were strangely silent. As if they suspected something they didn't quite want to know. It was better this way, she thought. She would explain when they were on their way. But she would have to be careful with Robin. There was no time to deal with a tantrum, and no way to promise the child new dolls where they were going. Robin would need her old friends. Jessie said she would try to think of a way they could take everything. There was a small rubber raft in the garage; perhaps they could tie it behind the canoe, like a trailer. If it was loaded carefully, the weight evenly distributed and strapped down securely with a piece of canvas, it might not be too heavy to pull. Hard to steer, though, even with real paddles. Luckily there were real paddles in the garage; they would not have to use Diane's crude pole. But it would be tricky, and they would be moving very slowly. Jessie wanted to be on Reef Island before the patrol boats began cruising the bay.

Finally she decided to risk it. With a trailer, Jessie could take a few things, too. Her paint box and some rolled-up canvases, drawing pads, an easel. It would be nice to have those, and there was no telling when they could afford to buy such luxuries. She could not touch the money in her bank account or use a credit card if Jessie Waterman did not exist. She had a couple of pieces of good jewelry; she could pry the stones loose and sell those somehow. Have to throw the settings away—settings could be traced. In the meantime she had about three hundred dollars in cash, including the hundred Kate had lent her. She had not wanted to take that, but she knew she would need it. *Kate.* Would she never stop thinking of Kate? Kate gone. So beautiful in the steel-gray predawn light, with her long dark hair streaming behind her in the wind. They had walked together to the edge of town. Like walking into a nightmare. Huge white emergency searchlight beaming up from the flooded main street, like a huge empty face, a dead Cyclopean eye, upturned from the wreckage as if it couldn't bear to look down. The long line of survivors, weeping or mute with shock, huddled outside the police station and the village records office, waiting for instructions, for news, for shelter, for someone to explain what had happened to them.

Thick foliage filled the streets—enormous ragged stumps

and tops of magnificent trees that had stood for generations, now prostrate in the road like discarded Christmas decorations. And everywhere the armed guards, patrolling, rifles resting across their hips, anticipating other kinds of trouble.

They had wheeled in emergency power generators and trucks with portable coffee-dispensing machines. Stalled automobiles and trucks seemed to be floating, their headlights on, peering dazedly above the waterline. One of the summer hotels had opened for the occasion; it had a cheery fire going in the lounge, and the flicker of it was visible from outside. Through the window one could see people warming themselves, shaking the fear off their bodies.

Highway crews were already at work, hauling the tree carcasses off the roads. There was a bus loading at the bus station, bound for Centerville, some fifteen miles in toward the city. Trains were running in Centerville. There would be no trains to or from Andrea Island for days, possibly weeks; the tracks had been washed away. The bus was half empty; there would be nothing else leaving until late morning. Kate glanced at Jessie and got on. She sat next to a window, pressing her small white face against the glass.

B. G. stood in the crowd across the street, clenching and unclenching his fists, resisting the urge to climb on that bus and get her. Claim what was rightfully his. Kate, he sighed, once, and then turned away. Kate turned away, too, fixing her eyes on the back of the driver's neck, on the windshield, the headlights of the bus gleaming palely across the dark wet road. I'm going home, she thought. I'm free of you, B. G. She turned again toward the window and gazed at her reflection. Liar, she whispered.

They found two big plastic tablecloths that said *Picnic!* on them in five different languages, and used them to cover their precious cargo, tying it securely to the raft with heavy ropes. Robin eyed the lumpy results distrustfully, and at the last minute insisted on untying one corner to get Hatshepsut and Charlotte out. If Hatshepsut got wet, she argued, her sacred eye paint would run, making her susceptible to mysterious eye infections. As for Charlotte, the epoxy attaching her new head to her old neck was not yet dry. Robin would carry both dolls inside her sweater.

Finally they pushed off, Jessie wading out until the water was up to her shoulders, carefully pulling the little canoe by a rope attached to its bow. The raft bobbed along behind, with Diane leaning out of the boat to push wreckage out of its way with one of the paddles. Jessie held her breath. What they needed least in the world at this moment was a sharp stick slicing into the rubberized underbelly of their pioneer vessel.

When it seemed safe, Jessie let go of the rope, gave the canoe a last gentle push outward, and climbed in. She began to paddle with strong, careful strokes, keeping one wary eye on the shoreline for early patrol boats. She felt like a spy invading enemy waters. This orange canoe was like a beacon signaling COME AND GET ME.

Diane lay huddled on the floor, wrapped in blankets and sweaters, her head between Jessie's legs. Robin sat at the bow, scouting the water ahead for dangerous floating objects and sharp rocks.

They had been moving steadily and in silence for nearly an hour when Robin turned her head suddenly and said, Will Daddy find us?

Jessie hesitated and then said, carefully, I don't know, Robin. She told herself it was unfortunately true.

I hope nobody finds us, Diane said. She hadn't meant to say that; it just popped out. Robin's head was still turned; she stared at her sister. I'd have no Daddy, she said.

You'd have Jessie, Diane replied, matter-of-factly. And me.

Robin considered that for a moment, and let it pass. Is Kate coming back? she asked. Diane turned to look at Jessie, still paddling silently. Is she?

149

I don't know, Jessie said again, avoiding their eyes.

You want her to, said Robin. It was not a question.

Kate doesn't belong with us, said Diane coldly.

What makes you say that? Jessie asked lightly.

If she belonged with us, she wouldn't have left. She didn't even say goodbye.

You were both sleeping, Jessie said. Kate didn't—I wouldn't let her disturb you.

She wouldn't have left like that, Diane said, unshaken.

Sometimes, said Jessie softly, people aren't so sure where they belong.

You are, said Robin.

Jessie smiled. I didn't used to be. I only just—

We're not going back to the city ever, said Robin. Are we?

No, said Diane, we're islanders now. Right? Jessie didn't answer.

Islanders? Robin frowned. Sounds like we're foreign.

We are, said Diane. We came from the eye of a hurricane, didn't we? Refugees!

Jessie fished the navigational map out of her sweater pocket and handed it to Diane. See the red circle? she said. That's where we're going.

Reef Island, said Diane solemnly, and passed the map forward to Robin.

Reef Island, Robin echoed.

We're going to learn how to fish for scallops, said Jessie.

We're going to stay there? Robin said. Always?

Stay there, said Jessie. I don't know how long always is. We'll see if we like it.

I don't like scallops, said Robin.

You will, said Jessie. She began to paddle faster. They were quite far out now, safely out of sight from the shoreline, and well beyond the drifting wreckage. She looked up at the lightening sky and smiled. Minerva was dead. Jessie Waterman too. But they were going to make it.

Two weeks after Hurricane Minerva, the official toll of casualties stood at 34 dead, 9 missing. The tragic disappearance of Jessie Waterman and her two young daughters had been a featured highlight of the storm coverage on television, in newspapers and magazines, primarily because the story could be built around dazzling photographs of Jessie as a model, culled from old and well-known advertisements in which her memorable face had sold famous brands of perfume, cosmetics and extravagant clothes. The fact that the Waterman cottage was the only one left standing on the far end of the island added another touching, ironic note. Altogether, it made a perfect little human-interest postscript to the major news about property damage and the marshaling of forces to clean up the devastation: "Life on Andrea Island —goes on."

Roy flew back from Copenhagen the day after the Andrea Island police notified him that no trace had been found, though of course Coast Guard boats were still patrolling the bay area. They did not use the term "dragging." In the meantime, the names of Jessie, Diane and Robin Waterman had already been released as among those "missing." Unfortunately, no recent photographs of the children were available to help the searchers. Diane's mother had furnished an old school portrait of Diane as a chubby eleven-year-old, and the family's city friends had managed to unearth a picture of Robin in a pink dress and a little paper hat, taken the previous year at a friend's birthday party. Roy himself had an assortment of baby pictures in his apartment, but he couldn't even say for sure which of his many babies was which, not that it would have helped. On the other hand, if the police had wanted any more photographs of Jessie, he could have given them another thousand.

The two weeks passed before Roy could bring himself to fly out to the island from the city, to look at the house and clear out their things. He had not spoken to Kate Saville since that first morning after the hurricane struck, when the news reached him in Europe. He had called her then in the city, called her frantically that whole day, before she answered her telephone.

It had occurred to him that there was an outside chance Jessie and the girls had gone into town with Kate, might even be staying with her. Out shopping . . . but as the telephone rang unanswered hour after hour, he began to wonder whether Kate too might be among the missing. When she finally picked up the phone, he was actually furious that she had been merely out, leading some presumably normal existence. *Where the hell have you been?* he shouted at her. She was so stunned to hear his voice that she barely heard what he said, or how. Yet she had been steeling herself for this call. Dreading it since the moment she stepped aboard the bus at Andrea Island.

I've been out, she said in an odd, strained little voice. Guilty.

I *know* that, for God's sake! he yelled. I've been calling you since dawn. Did you know Jessie and the girls are missing? When did you leave there?

Kate took a deep breath and closed her eyes. Sunday, she said. They were fine, Sunday. Oh, God, she wanted to hang up. To be disconnected.

Were they going anywhere, that you know of? Sunday? Or any time—was she planning—?

No, Kate cut in, I don't know anything. Listen, Roy, please, it's—I'm exhausted; I can't talk any more now.

You're *exhausted?* he shouted in disbelief. I'm trying—

I know, she said quickly. I've been worried sick, too. I hope they, that it's all just some mix-up or something, and they'll turn up . . . uh, when are you coming back?

Tomorrow, he said, couldn't get a plane before—listen, Kate, did they—I mean did they take walks along the beach or anything? Did she walk into town to shop?

I don't know, Roy, she answered dully. I mean, yes, they took walks sometimes. Different places. Roy, you're really upsetting me—

I'm sorry, he said, unconvincingly. Is something wrong? You do sound—peculiar.

She would have to play it out now. He was not going to let her off. She might have known he wouldn't. Of course something's wrong, she said, trying to sound angry instead of . . . peculiar. My best friend's missing, maybe dead, and you're grilling me on the phone as if I were a—suspect in a murder case. What do you want from me, Roy? *I don't know anything!* I left *Sunday,* and they were *fine* Sunday. I never heard from them after that.

It didn't work. What time, he said relentlessly, did you leave, Sunday?

I don't know! she cried. I don't remember! Sometime in the afternoon.

By train? Yes, she said. No. I mean I got a lift . . . with friends.

They came to pick you up? At the house?

She couldn't think any more. Kate? he said. You still there?

I went, she said, to meet them. Him. I stayed with him, until . . . her voice trailed off.

Roy would have gone on asking who, where . . . but he stopped abruptly. Maybe he was being unfair. I'm sorry, he said, trying for gentleness. It came out only a little less than gruff. It's just that you were the last person who saw them—

She sensed that he wanted to pull back, finally. If she could just hold on another minute. I understand, Roy. It's painful for me too. I . . . love Jessie, too, you know. I just don't know what more I can tell you.

If only, he said, you could remember, anything she said— give us something to go on, help those idiots look in the right *places,* at least.

Suddenly Kate said, They're not going to find her, Roy.

What?

Don't you see, she said, racing now, reckless, it's hopeless. If they were alive they'd have turned up by now.

Roy was enraged. You're incredible, he said. You're not real.

They may never, she said carefully, find anything. Bodies. Sometimes they just . . . the boats just keep scouring the area, and they never . . . Face it, Roy, they'd have been found if they were going to be found. Give it up.

Thanks, Kate, he said icily. I'll see you.

Chapter 16

IT WAS DARK when Roy drove out to the house from the village office, accompanied by a deputy chief of police and a coastguardsman. Don't know as how you'll see much tonight, the police chief had said. Ought to wait till morning; no power on out there yet.

I know, said Roy, I'm staying over at the inn; I'll go out again tomorrow. I just wanted—to see it—you know. . . . The police chief nodded. These last weeks he'd done a fair amount of this sort of thing.

Sure is a mess, said the coastguardsman, surveying the living room. The ceiling had caved in, and the smell of rotted upholstery was overpowering. Everything was covered with a thin white film, like new-fallen snow. Dried salt.

Amazing it's still standing, said the police chief. Foundation's gone. Better be careful where you step. He shined his big flashlight around the room. Looks like they really tried to protect themselves, Roy said. Look at this—she barricaded the windows.

They put up a good fight, all right, said the police chief. Woman alone, two little kids.

The coastguardsman's mouth opened as if he were about to say something. He changed his mind and closed it.

Damn shame, said the police chief.

Roy said, Someone actually checked every house here while the storm was still—?

That's right, sir, said the coastguardsman. I was stationed at the tower over at the point when she started. Checked them all—all that were still standing then.

And nobody was here. In the middle of the afternoon.

That's right, sir. Nobody.

Roy shook his head. Wonder how she knew to put up those boards and all, ahead of time. And if she heard storm warnings, why she'd do that and then go out? With the two kids . . . ? Makes no sense.

What time about, did you get here? the police chief asked the coastguardsman.

I don't recall exactly, sir. Before the eye passed, I know that.

Puts it between one o'clock and three, say? The tower went around noon, didn't it?

The coastguardsman nodded, uncomfortable. Guess that's about as close as we can come, sir. I was kind of—he laughed—busy.

Roy was examining the door leading to the garage. The massive dining room table, nailed up against metal supports. How could she—? Suddenly there was an incredible noise, an explosion of whirring and chopping, like a machine gun. It was coming from the garage. The three of them raced out the front door and around to the driveway. Roy began pounding at the garage door. The others pounded, too, until it gave way. The noise was deafening. The police chief flashed his light around: wreckage, still floating in water. Rats. In the corner, an electric drill, plugged into a wall, had suddenly come alive and gone berserk, skidding wildly through an enormous pile of wood and metal scraps. Power's been restored, the police chief said, heaving a sigh of obvious relief. See, there's a light on in that storage closet. Someone must have been drilling down there when the lights went out. Better not go in; it's a death trap, electricity on and all that water.

They walked back to the front of the house and went in to shut off the circuit breakers.

Heavy carpentry work, Roy said, shaking his head in bewilderment. Jessie never, in her whole life—drilling—

Times like that, said the coastguardsman, people do the weirdest things. Had a woman over on Collins Hill, little bit of a thing, lifted a twenty-foot elm tree off her husband's leg. After the storm, she couldn't believe she did it. Woman about a hundred and ten pounds.

Roy wasn't listening. The police chief's flashlight had illuminated a pile of papers on the floor of the dining room. He went over to look at them. Maps. Detailed local navigational maps. Anybody ever check all those little islands up in North Bay? he asked. Couldn't someone get carried six, eight miles from here? Wash up on one of those empty beaches? What about in a boat? Suppose they got hold of a boat somehow—there were loose boats drifting all over the place, weren't there?

The police chief was tired. Possible, he said, stifling a yawn. Most of 'em been checked out, though, those little islands.

Most—not all?

Still checking, said the coastguardsman defensively.

Could I—would it be possible to go along? On one of your boats? Roy said. Tomorrow?

Don't see why not, said the police chief. Bailey here could take you, if his commander okays it. Right, Bailey?

Happy to, said Bailey.

Reef Island had been a prototypical shantytown before Minerva struck. Now it was a watery slum. Two-thirds of the fishermen's shacks had been destroyed, and unlike Andrea

Island, there was no sign here of any valiant effort to clean up, much less rebuild.

Rubble still lay in the front yards of houses, and gardens were covered with debris and filth. Buildings were hastily patched the morning after the storm and left that way, eyesores that would hardly stand through the rough island winter. Whenever there was a light breeze, chunks of wood and metal blew through the streets. People walked with their shoulders hunched up and their heads down—even the children.

Part of the problem was that Reef Island couldn't decide where to start. When the storm had passed, leaving the town a shambles, the village board issued regulations banning all building projects, except for emergency roofing jobs or makeshift temporary repairs, until the town could pass a new building code.

Then the island's appeal for state and county funds was being held up, so that no work could start on streets or public buildings. Banks and relief agencies had come through with help for some of the fishermen, enabling them to buy new boats or fix up their old ones, but their families continued to camp out under the patched floorboards of raised houses, or in abandoned trailers that had been set up by relief agencies as temporary shelters in the immediate wake of the storm.

There were other troubles too. State, local and county officials began squabbling over who was responsible for different phases of the relief program, so that dazed families were shunted from one agency to another for help, and finally gave up trying. Construction workers were threatening to strike over pay and working conditions. There was only one doctor left on the island—the other two had moved out after the storm—and several teachers had fled, too, leaving a severe staff shortage in the school.

The Reef Island art colony, a handful of painters whose houses were clustered just outside the town and whose families had little to do with the life of the island, seemed to be the only group that had weathered the storm; from where they lived, the decline of Reef Island seemed scarcely noticeable. They had repaired their houses themselves, most of them within a day or two, without bothering to file plans or hire construction workers. A few of these families had been airlifted out after the hurricane, but most of them had returned. There was also one new family in their midst, a man who had moved in quietly with his two young children a day or so after the storm. Their house was up on a cliff, set apart from the others, and badly damaged. It was said he had leased it for the winter for two hundred dollars, with the agreement that he would make all the necessary repairs. The owner of the house, a man from Centerville who never used the place winters, had been delighted with the arrangement. It saved him from dealing with either the building codes or the labor unions, and he wouldn't even have to come out and supervise the work.

The new man kept to himself mostly, though his daughters attended the school and he had occasional visitors from the town—a series of young women who came and stayed for brief periods. There was some talk about him, of course, but nobody really knew much. At first it had been assumed he was a builder, and then it was thought he might be an artist. He was seen early every morning, out on the rocks, painting. About four or five days after he moved in, it was reported that he had salvaged one of the damaged fishing boats that had been blown ashore and abandoned during the storm. After that he went out every morning with his kids, working the fish traps, and painted only in the late afternoon, around sunset. By then nobody could quite decide whether he was an artist who fished for relaxation, a builder who had taken up painting, or a fisherman. . . . On Reef Island, especially after Minerva, nobody much cared.

Chapter 17

THE COAST GUARD CUTTER pulled ashore, and Surfman Bailey got out to make inquiries at the town office. No bodies had washed up there except for those of two local fishermen whose boat had been lost in the storm. There was one new family on the island, fellow moved over from Andrea Island after he lost his wife, his house and his boat.

Roy Waterman showed the town clerks a photograph of Jessie. They shook their heads. Nope. Sure must have been a fine-looking woman, though. Damn shame.

Want to go talk to the new fellow up the cove? the clerk asked helpfully. He checked his records. Name of Kilroy. B. G. Kilroy.

Funny name, said Roy, with a weary smile. Guess there's no point in going up there, though, thanks.

Surfman Bailey shrugged. Suit yourself. Well, said Roy, reconsidering, let's go talk to him—just for the hell of it. Only take a few minutes.

Mr. Kilroy? said Leo Bailey. Sorry to bother you, sir, but we're looking for someone, storm victims, thought you might be of some help. Woman and kids lost off Andrea Island.

Roy Waterman was peering past the coastguardsman, into the house. Mess. Typical filthy artist's shack. Smelled of fish and women. B. G. stared at them for an instant, and then stood aside to let them in. His children were out on the boat, he mumbled, and his woman was downtown buying something. They always down buying something, ain't they? He laughed.

Roy pulled out his picture of Jessie. It was a beautiful head shot, Roy's favorite from the set that had been made for her most famous perfume ad—the perfume they had finally named Jessie, because it seemed to match her. B. G. held the picture in his hand. Nice, he said. Real nice. Too bad—

We wondered, said Roy uncomfortably, if you might have seen her on Andrea Island, anywhere, before the storm. What part of the island were you on, yourself?

Collins Hill, said B. G. Roof and front of the house blew clean off. Lost my woman too. His voice seemed on the edge of breaking.

I'm sorry, said Roy. B. G. Kilroy shrugged. They's other fish—

Well, said Bailey, sorry to bother you.

As they turned to go, Roy's foot struck a doll that was half hidden behind the door. He picked it up. A queen doll, only with a beard. Egyptian or something. Interesting, he said, handing it to B. G. My little girl used to—

B. G. held out his hand for the doll. Their eyes met briefly; there was no sign of recognition. Hope you find . . . what you missing, man, said B. G.

Thanks, said Roy. B. G. watched them retreat down the path from his house and board the cutter. He smiled. Shit, he said. Some people got real trouble. Makes me feel lucky. Feel like a new man.

Kate Saville had not readjusted well to city life. She had all the ordinary symptoms of displaced personhood—lack of sleep, appetite, libido, ability to concentrate. Nothing serious, she kept telling herself. Nothing a good suicide wouldn't fix.

Every night before going to bed she stared at herself in the bathroom mirror and said, Now you go right to sleep and don't think about B. G. Don't think about little islands. Don't think. . . . Then she would lie awake all night, disobeying.

Often she felt his eyes on her in the street, on buses or in elevators. She would turn around and see no one, or someone else. Damn spook, she would curse at him, forcing herself to laugh at that, because it hurt so much.

More than three weeks had passed when she decided to call Roy Waterman, for no reason. No reason she would care to admit.

Hi, she said. How are you?

Kate? he said. He was not glad to hear from her.

Just thought I'd call to see how you are—

He didn't answer.

—and ask you how things went—out there, I mean.

Nothing, he said coldly. Not a thing. House was wrecked. I met a nice coastguardsman and some cops, and a fair number of other people who were just about as helpful as you. I also took a complete tour of the outer islands. Depressing as hell. Especially I don't recommend Reef Island.

Reef? That nice little fishing town? With the artists' colony?

Used to be, maybe, said Roy. You never saw anything so awful. As if the whole place expected to wake up dead, and they're disappointed.

Terrible, said Kate. What made you go there?

I don't know. Some guy from Andrea Island washed up there. I talked to him. I talked to maybe fifty guys who washed up fifty different places. Nothing. She just . . . His voice trailed off.

There was a sudden tingling sensation on the back of Kate's

neck. Reef Island. I'm really sorry, Roy, Kate said. About everything. You know.
Thanks for calling, he said.
If there's anything—
There isn't, he said. Isn't anything.

It was New Year's Day when Kate Saville reached Reef Island, and found her way to the house on the cliff. B. G. Kilroy, it said on the mailbox. B. G. Kilroy, she said aloud, and knocked on the door. Robin answered. Oh, she said, it's you. Hi. She smiled shyly. B. G. and Diane are out catching dinner. Kate smiled back. I'll wait, she said.